"Perha
why I

Smug amusement colored Meredith's voice. She was leaning against the bathroom door, her arms full of towels. Brandt's terry robe hung on a hook behind her.

Startled, Brandt combed his hair away from his face. Water dripped off his head and beaded on his shoulders. Rivulets trickled over his chest and downward; Meredith watched their progress. With spurious calm he asked, "Will you hand me my robe, please?"

She shook her head.

"At least give me something to dry off with." Brandt felt his body stirring under her inspection.

"No."

He stepped toward her, bare feet squishing on the sodden bath mat. She retreated a step. "Dammit, Meredith, stop playing games. I'm cold!"

Her smile broadened and she raised her eyebrows. "Don't bluster, darling, it doesn't work when you're naked. Besides, I'm definitely not here to play games...."

Lynda Ward moved to California as a child, married at eighteen and had three sons. Somehow she also managed to attend college, but abandoned her music program when her lifelong love— writing—began to pay off. She sold her first book to Harlequin in 1981. Before that, she'd had more than a dozen short stories published—one about a woman who falls in love with the pilot of a UFO!

With her fertile imagaination, Lynda continues to come up with fresh story ideas, and *Love in Tandem* is a prime example.

Books by Lynda Ward

Love in Tandem

LYNDA WARD

Harlequin Books

TORONTO • NEW YORK • LONDON
AMSTERDAM • PARIS • SYDNEY • HAMBURG
STOCKHOLM • ATHENS • TOKYO • MILAN

The Dixieland Jubilee described in this story is
sponsored each Memorial weekend by the
Sacramento Traditional Jazz Society.
Nobody does it better.

Published February 1987

ISBN 0-373-25241-2

1

"OH, LORD, are you all right?"

Meredith Forrester's shout of dismay echoed along the rows of parked cars. Almost tripping on her high heels, she jumped down from the stalled van, slamming the door behind her. She scurried to the aid of the man who lay sprawled on the asphalt, tangled in the frame of a lightweight bicycle. One wheel of his ten-speed rotated freely, bright April sunlight flashing on the spokes, but he did not move.

Fear left a coppery taste in her mouth as she stared down at him. He was so still. He didn't look hurt, though. She couldn't see his face because his foam-plastic helmet had slipped over his forehead, but his chest moved rhythmically beneath a T-shirt bearing the logo of a Sacramento cycling club. The long muscular legs, bulging thighs displayed by brief shorts, appeared unbruised. His knees weren't even scraped. Surely—please, dear Lord—he was only winded.

Biting her lip, Meredith gauged the distance between the rusty bumper of the vehicle and the lean body on the pavement. She'd been inching her brother's battle-scarred panel truck along the lanes of the packed parking lot that lay between the boxy concrete office building and the tree-covered river levee. As it was the middle of a Friday morning, there'd been no one else moving around when she first pulled in and began her search for a vacant space.

The only two empty slots she found were marked reserved.

She had almost given up in despair when, without
warning, the man on the bicycle had raced into her path.
Having swerved instantly, she'd been certain she'd missed
him; it was only panic that had made him skid, falling in
a heap. But now she wondered if perhaps the fender had
brushed against him after all.

Heedless of her nylons or the narrow skirt of her beige
suit, she dropped to her knees on the pavement beside the
man. Brushing back a long strand of bright red hair that
had escaped from her sleek French twist, she adjusted her
glasses in a habitual gesture of nervousness as she studied
him. Without seeing his face, she couldn't guess how old
he was, but he had a good—a damned good—body, hard
and athletic. His sweat-dampened shirt clung to his chest,
outlining bone and firm muscle. The clean, musky odor
of him, an intimate fragrance, teased her nostrils provocatively. It was a long time since Meredith had been close
enough to a man to be aware of his scent. Leaning over
him, she brushed his arm with her leg. She poked his
shoulder gingerly. "P-please," she stammered, her usually melodious voice rasping with dread, "are you all
right?"

The instant she made contact with his arm, a hand
lashed out. Strong fingers encased by a leather and cloth-
mesh glove snaked upward and caught her wrist. Meredith rocked back reflexively. She could feel the tremor in
his hand, but when she tried to pull her arm away, his grip
tightened.

Helplessly she watched him lever himself upright. With
his other hand he unsnapped the chin strap from his safety
helmet and shoved it off his forehead. A thick pelt of sun-
streaked blond hair was revealed, then a tanned, sharply

planed face with high cheekbones and a square jaw. There was a cleft in his chin that seemed to invite a woman to sip nectar from it.

He appeared to be somewhere in his early thirties, definitely in his prime. *Oh, my*, Meredith thought, startled and bemused by the sheer physical pleasure she felt just looking at him. Her fears redoubled; even if the accident had been his fault, she hated to think of anything so beautiful being damaged.

When he looked at her, Meredith's apprehension faded. All at once she knew why the man had lain so still on the blacktop—he was absolutely rigid with outrage.

Nordic-blue eyes glared. Beneath a lavish guardsman's mustache, his lips lost their sensual curve as he ground out, "Damn it, lady, why the hell don't you watch where you're going!"

Meredith gaped. "*Me* watch?" she choked, flabbergasted by his attack. "Now, wait a minute—you rode right out in front of me!"

"If you hadn't been racing down the aisle—"

"I was going barely five miles an hour!"

"Listen—"

Her concern vanished in a blaze of indignation. "No, you listen. You zoomed out from between a couple of cars—"

"I came off the bike trail," he informed her impatiently, nodding toward the spot where he'd appeared.

Meredith looked again and for the first time noticed a narrow spur of pavement that dropped down from the rise of the levee and abutted onto the parking lot. Stripes painted on the asphalt indicated the point where it emptied into the traffic lane.

"Everyone knows to keep an eye open for bicycles when they drive past here," the man continued.

"Since I've never been in this parking lot before, I had no way of knowing about the crossing," Meredith retorted. "There ought to be a sign or something. As it is, you're lucky I was able to miss you."

The man glanced disdainfully toward the van with its battered, primer-dotted body. "Yeah, I guess you're right, at that. From the looks of that relic you're driving, you don't miss very often."

Meredith's eyes glinted. "I have been driving since I was sixteen," she informed him icily, "and in all those eight years I've never received so much as a parking—" She broke off, suddenly remembering the cassette she'd flipped over in the dashboard tape deck just before the rider materialized in front of her. Her eyes *might* have been momentarily averted from the road.... She felt heat surge upward from her throat, causing her translucent cheeks to glow like neon. "Oh, hell," she muttered.

"You were saying..."

Meredith clenched her teeth. It was infuriating to have a complexion that displayed her emotions like a mood ring. Worse, she knew the crimson painting her face would make her freckles, carefully hidden beneath makeup, blaze into prominence. Her bronze-spattered skin had been the bane of her existence since childhood. She'd attended a dozen different schools, and every one of them had sheltered some bully who called her Spot or Pinto. Sometimes the hateful sobriquets had stuck. As an adult, Meredith was no longer called names, but the problem still existed, silent but insidious. People—such as the cyclist at her feet—never seemed to take a freckled redhead seriously.

Making an effort to act with dignity she admitted, "All right. Although I still think you were the one at fault, it's possible I looked away from the road for a second. I was listening to Billie Holiday, and—"

"Billie Holiday?" he exclaimed in surprise. "You have good taste in music." At this discovery, his mood seemed to shift. He studied Meredith thoughtfully, then glanced sidelong at the van. "Look," he ventured, "I think we were probably both a little careless. Maybe that's not important. What is important is, are *you* all right? That heap doesn't look particularly safe to drive."

"I'm all right," Meredith said, not looking at him. She knew he was right about the truck, but family loyalty prevented her from agreeing aloud.

The vehicle was a disgrace and an eyesore, unfit to be on the road. But, damn it, it wasn't hers! The truck belonged to her older brother, and despite being the dearest man in the world, Mike's attitude toward driving could only be described as offhand. In fact, that was his attitude toward everything except Meredith and music. All he required of an automobile was that it be big enough to haul the band and their instruments from one gig to the next. His indifference showed. Were it not for the fact that a couple of the other musicians were handy with tools, Mike's clunker probably would have ended up in the junkyard years ago.

At the moment her brother was in San Francisco, following up on a demo tape he'd sent an advertising agency. Before departing on the two-hundred-mile round trip, even Mike had acknowledged the limitations of his van, so he'd asked Meredith if he could borrow her neat compact sedan for the day. She had agreed only with great reluctance, praying her Toyota—not to mention Mike—would survive the journey.

Looking down, she noticed that the cyclist's fingers were still wrapped around her wrist. With dismay she also became aware that her skirt had ridden high up on her legs, displaying most of her thighs. Her blush deepened. Trying awkwardly to maintain her balance, she clamped her knees together and tugged at the hem with her free hand. "Will you please let go of me?" she asked with strained courtesy. "I'd like to stand up."

Beneath the blond mustache the man's lips quirked. "Why?" he murmured. "The view down here is so pleasant." His gaze lingered on the sleek curve of her hips before skimming upward over her body. "In fact," he added appreciatively, his eyes dwelling on her trim waist and the gentle curve of her breast, "the view is pretty good all over."

He paused, and Meredith held her breath, unsure whether she was offended or aroused by his sensual provocation. She reminded herself sternly that as gorgeous as the man was, he was also a total stranger. And if there was one lesson she'd learned during her years on the stage, it was to be cautious around strangers. She waited.

When Meredith did not stir, the man's eyes at last continued their upward course. As he stared into her face, he frowned. "Don't I know you from somewhere?"

Meredith's brows lifted. She'd expected a more original line. On the other hand, she admitted he did sound genuinely puzzled. Deciding to accept the remark at face value, she replied, "No, we've never met." With silent conviction she added, *Believe me, I'd remember.*

The man appeared unconvinced. "But I'm sure..." While he studied her, his grip relaxed.

Feeling the tension ease, Meredith jerked free and jumped to her feet. "If you'll excuse me," she said breathlessly, "I must be going. I have an appointment."

He rose with agile grace, and Meredith noted that he was taller than she'd have guessed, perhaps six-two or

-three. Stripping off his cycling gloves, he inquired casually, "Aren't we supposed to exchange names and phone numbers? For insurance purposes, I mean."

Meredith shook her head. She tried not to stare at those long bronzed legs, that powerful torso. She knew she was behaving like an idiot, but she couldn't remember ever feeling so flustered by a man before. And not even during her first intense romance with a history instructor at the university had she felt this kind of arousal. Her reaction stunned and troubled her.

With an effort Meredith garnered her composure. She couldn't waste time here; she had important business to conduct at Warcom. "I don't think there's any need to report the accident." She chuckled weakly as she inched away. "Neither one of us appears to be hurt, thank goodness. Your bike seems okay, and heaven knows one more ding in this old van isn't going to make much difference.

"Forget the bike. I'd feel better if I could check on you later," he insisted. "You do seem a little shaken."

You'll never know the half of it, Meredith thought wryly, but before she could speak, the side door of the building flew open.

A dozen preschool-age children tumbled out, squealing and running in all directions. A young woman followed, looking faintly harried. "Hey, you're supposed to stay in line!" she shouted, but one of her charges dashed into the parking lot, intent on some invisible goal.

Swooping down, the cyclist caught the little boy around the waist. "Hey, you," he growled with mock severity, "where do you think you're going?"

"I spotted a butterfly," the child responded matter-of-factly, unintimidated. "It was pretty, and I was gonna catch it."

The man's expression softened magically. "Don't you think it would be better to let the butterfly go so that it can keep flying around and everyone can appreciate how pretty it is? Besides, right now, you're supposed to mind your teacher." Without waiting for an answer, he hoisted the child onto his shoulder and marched him back toward the building.

Watching him stride away, Meredith shook herself irritably. She had no time to stand around gawking at this man, no matter how handsome he was. She ducked behind the steering wheel of the van and revved the engine, wincing as she ground the gears when she trundled away. In the rearview mirror she could see the man standing on the sidewalk in the center of a cluster of children. "Goodbye," she murmured, wondering why she bothered to speak aloud.

Meredith abandoned hope of finding a parking space in the lot and began to search for an opening on the street. By now she had pushed aside all thoughts of the cyclist; she was afraid she would be late for her appointment. She couldn't be late! Too much depended on this interview.

Half a block away from Warcom's main entrance she wheeled the van clumsily into the curb, hubcaps scraping against concrete. Grabbing her handbag, she yanked the keys from the ignition and started sprinting along the sidewalk.

At the entrance to the building she paused to catch her breath and smooth her hair. The formal styles she preferred for work required constant vigilance against the natural curl of her long tresses. When wispy tendrils had been tucked securely into her French twist once more, she gazed at the double glass doors in front of her.

Neat, unobtrusive gold lettering identified Warcom Electronics, one of the leading companies in California's rapidly growing high-tech industry. The name was not as familiar as those of some of the computer manufacturers glutting Silicon Valley, but it was still a name to be reckoned with. Unlike the companies that had sprung up like mushrooms after the advent of silicon-chip technology, Warcom was a long-established firm. Founded in the early sixties by Walter Warren and his partner, the company's growth had been slow but steady. At a time when newer businesses were beginning to cut back or even go under, Warcom remained remarkably sound, conservative and stable. It was exactly the sort of company in which Meredith had always dreamed of making a place for herself.

At last it looked as if that dream might come true. For the first time ever Meredith had a good chance of obtaining a job commensurate with her abilities. She was a gifted and intuitive mathematician, an honor student in college until family obligations had forced her to drop out without graduating. In the past, whenever she applied for jobs in her field, her lack of a degree had frustrated her. No matter how capable she was, personnel officers never seemed to look beyond that blank line on her resumé.

This time, however, she was going to bypass the personnel office and go directly to the top. In her purse she carried a glowing letter of recommendation from one of her college professors. Meredith had bumped into her at the supermarket a few days before. Shocked to learn that Meredith was wasting her talents working as a part-time bookkeeper, she had offered to contact a close personal friend who was looking for an assistant. Although Meredith was grateful for the professor's concern, she hadn't really expected anything to come of it. She'd been astounded and delighted two days later when Walter Warren's secretary called to arrange an interview.

As the elevator ascended to the fifth floor, Meredith squinted into her compact mirror one last time. When she dabbed powder on the freckles bridging her nose, her hand trembled. She hoped her nervousness wasn't too obvious; Mike had already commented on it that morning.

"Settle down, Merry," he had suggested, puzzled. "It's only an interview for some dreary desk job, you know."

Tucking the compact back into her purse, Meredith shook her head. How could she settle down? This wasn't any ordinary interview any more than it was a dreary job at stake. This was a chance for her to begin a challenging, satisfying career in her chosen field. She was afraid to admit how much she wanted it, for fear of tempting fate. Mike just didn't understand. Even as close as the two of them were, as much as he loved her, Mike's own ambitions were firmly fixed on the world of music, and he could never comprehend what mathematics meant to Meredith.

The elevator stopped with a chime. *B natural*, Meredith noted automatically. Stepping out into the empty corridor, she paused to get her bearings. Obviously this was the executive wing. Here there was no bare tile or utilitarian enamel paint such as she'd glimpsed downstairs. The long hall had wall-to-wall plush carpeting; the walls were covered by rich flocked paper and decorated with watercolor landscapes. Meredith's spirits rose. She'd always hoped to work in surroundings like this someday.

Recalling the receptionist's directions, Meredith turned right and headed for the golden oak doors at the end of the corridor. The place seemed deserted, but as she passed doors with engraved brass plaques—Ms Nakatani, Mr. Dahlberg—she could pick out the reassuring murmur of voices, the click of typewriters behind them.

"Ms Forrester? Oh, good. Mr. Warren's been waiting for you." Walter Warren's secretary was an effusive woman in her late forties, with stylishly frosted brown hair and a warm smile. The nameplate on her desk identified her as Lois Nelson.

Meredith adjusted her glasses and smiled shyly in answer to the cheerful greeting. Swallowing thickly, she asked, "I'm not late, am I? I had a little trouble on the way, and I was afraid—"

"Oh, no, my dear, you're right on time. Let me tell him you're here." She flipped the intercom switch and announced, "Sir, the young lady you were expecting has arrived. Shall I send her in?"

"Of course, Lois," boomed a disembodied male voice from the speaker. "By all means, send her in before she gets into a daze calculating the cube root of *pi* or something. Have to treat these geniuses delicately, you know."

"The only real genius I've ever met is you, boss. And sometimes I'm not sure you know the difference between *pi* and cake!" Lois Nelson bantered.

Through the speaker came a loud groan at the pun. With a chuckle Lois flicked off the intercom and grinned at Meredith, who was slightly dazed. "You can go in now, Ms Forrester." Noting Meredith's expression, she added kindly, "You mustn't mind Walter. He's a darling man, but he's also the world's most incorrigible tease. If you expect to work with him, you'll have to learn to give as good as you get."

Nodding weakly, Meredith said, "I-I'll try to remember that. Thank you." Bracing herself, she stepped through the door into the inner office.

She wasn't sure what she'd imagined the founder and head of a notable high-tech firm to look like, but she certainly hadn't expected a jovial giant with a fringe of grizzled hair and a full beard. The robust man rose to his feet behind a desk strewn with computer printouts. Meredith judged him to be about sixty years old and at least six-and-a-half feet tall. He wasn't wearing his suit coat, his tie was loose and his shirt sleeves were rolled back over sinewy arms. Meredith was reminded of a lumberjack uncomfortably decked out in his Sunday best, but there was nothing unsophisticated about the bright, intelligent eyes that glimmered in his seamed face.

He peered down at her. "Ms Forrester?" he greeted warmly, his large hand swallowing up the small one she held out. "I've been looking forward to meeting you."

"And I you," Meredith replied. "When my professor told me she had a friend who might have a job for me, I had no idea she meant you. I mean, the head of Warcom Electronics—" She sank into the chair he offered. Instantly she jumped again. Reaching gingerly behind her, her hazel eyes widened in astonishment when she discovered a set of plastic false teeth on the seat cushion.

"Oh, great, I wondered what had happened to those!" Walter exclaimed. Taking the teeth from Meredith, he wound them up and set them on the desk, where they chattered noisily, rustling the long sheets of fanfolded computer paper. When the spring ran down, Walter tucked the toy into a drawer and said calmly, "Now, why don't you tell me a little about yourself? I understand you were an honor student in college until you dropped out."

"Yes, sir," Meredith said wistfully, remembering her abortive stint at the local campus of the state university. She had loved her studies, working toward an advanced degree in applied mathematics, but her plans had changed during her junior year. One night she'd come home from a date to find Mike lying in a drunken stupor on the sofa, his prized collection of Bix Beiderbecke recordings in shards, strewn around the apartment. Suddenly she'd realized just how very frustrated and unhappy her brother was.

With an effort Meredith explained, "Family obligations made it necessary for me to drop out. My older brother had raised me from the time I was thirteen, when our parents died. My college tuition was paid by a scholarship I'd won, but Mike was still providing my room and board. There came a point in my life when I realized I just couldn't ask him to continue doing that for me, so I dropped out of school and enlisted with a temporary employment agency. Because of my bookkeeping skills I'm almost always busy—especially during the income tax season—but what I really want is a steady job with a future."

Walter listened in silence, and Meredith fumbled with the clasp on her purse. Drawing out a long white envelope, she handed it to Walter. "Here's the letter of recommendation the professor was kind enough to write, if you'd like to see it."

Walter waved one hand dismissively. "It's not necessary. When she telephoned, she told me that despite your lack of a degree, you were one of the most insightful mathematicians she'd ever met."

"I do love working with real numbers-statistics, technical analysis, business applications," Meredith replied, embarrassed by such high praise.

Nodding approvingly, Walter said, "Yes, that's what my friend indicated. She also told me I'd be a fool to let one of my competitors find you first. That's all the recommendation I need. However, you ought to save the letter for Brandt. I'm sure he'll want to take a look at it."

Meredith frowned. "Brandt? Who's he?"

"Brandt Dahlberg, my second in command," Walter elaborated. "His late father was my first partner. He handled finances, I was in charge of research and development. After he died twelve years ago, Brandt took his place. The boy's been like a son to me ever since. He's a fine, capable businessman, with enough training in engineering to keep on top of things around here. When I'm ready to retire, I'll be able to hand over the reins to him with confidence.

"His one weakness is that he doesn't have the academic background to deal with the kind of abstruse algorithms that are an integral part of high tech R and D. We've always compensated for that deficiency by making sure his personal assistant could handle the theoretical side of things." He paused, grimacing, and stroked his beard. "Unfortunately, the guy who's been Brandt's PA for the past three years suddenly decided to renounce the world and move to some ashram in Oregon. He left without notice, and now Brandt's desperate for a replacement. That's where you come in."

"Then I wouldn't be working with you?" Meredith asked, vaguely disappointed. She'd taken an instant liking to this genial bear of a man, with his bright eyes and silly toys. She felt sure he'd make a good boss.

Walter laughed and shook his head. "Oh, no, my dear. I apologize for any misunderstanding, but Brandt's the one who's looking for an assistant. I work alone, partly by preference and partly because the only person who could ever put up with my awful sophomoric sense of humor is Lois Nelson—and she's too darn valuable a secretary to waste in the lab!" He glanced at his wristwatch, puzzled. "Although I agreed to help screen candidates, the final choice is Brandt's. I can't imagine what's delayed him. I expected him long before—"

He was interrupted by the sound of the office door opening. Looking past Meredith, he called with relief,

"Oh, there you are, Brandt! I was beginning to think something had happened to you."

There was a deep rumble of laughter. "Sorry I'm late, Walter, but something did happen to me. In fact, it's a miracle I'm alive to talk about it!" Meredith sat frozen, chills shivering along her spine as the all-too-familiar voice continued. "Here I was, innocently minding my own business, coming off the bike trail, when all of a sudden some dizzy redhead in a ramshackle delivery truck tried to run me down in the parking lot!"

2

OH, HELL, Brandt thought with dismay as a slim figure rose from the chair between him and Walter. Even from the back there was no mistaking that astonishing hair.

"I still say the accident was your fault," he heard her mutter. Beneath the prim beige suit he could see her spine straight and taut as a bowstring. When she picked up her purse, her delicate profile became visible, the clean lines marred by her glasses. She flashed a regretful smile at Walter.

"It was a pleasure to meet you, Mr. Warren. Thank you for your time, and I'm sorry we wasted it. You've been very kind." Her voice was pitched about two tones too high, as she fought tears.

Walter looked puzzled. "Wait a minute. I don't understand. What's going on?"

"There's nothing going on, sir. But obviously this interview is pointless." She shrugged and turned to leave, refusing to look directly at Brandt. Quickly he stepped between her and the door.

She had to halt or collide with him. Her nose was about three inches from the elegant knot of his striped tie, and Brandt was relieved he'd had a chance to shower before changing into his suit. At least the smell of sweat had been replaced by woodsy cologne.

She lifted her head, and hazel eyes glinted into his. "Please get out of my way."

Brandt took a deep breath. "Look, I'm sorry," he said stiltedly. "I had no idea you were here, and I certainly had no intention of being rude. Please accept my apology, Mrs.—" He glanced at her left hand. "Ms—"

At the desk Walter exploded testily, "Brandt, Ms Forrester, will one of you kindly explain what's happening?"

"It's simple. As much as I'd love the job, I'm sure Mr. Dahlberg will prefer not to have a dizzy redhead as his personal assistant."

Damn. Brandt cursed silently as he realized for the first time exactly why the woman was in Walter's office. He shoved his hands into his pocket. "You're here to apply for the job as my assistant?"

"We've discussed the position, yes," Meredith informed him stiffly.

"Naturally the final decision is yours, Brandt," Walter put in, "but my first impressions are very favorable."

Mine, too, Brandt silently agreed. But being attractive was no qualification for the job that needed to be done. In fact, considering how closely they'd have to work together, this Ms Forrester's looks might even prove a detriment, perhaps severely testing his concentration. Nodding toward the chair Meredith had just vacated, Brandt suggested, "Well, then, why don't you sit down again and tell me about yourself? I suppose a good place to begin would be with your education. I assume you have at least a bachelor's degree in mathematics. Where did you earn it?"

Meredith's hopes plummeted once again. "I'm afraid I didn't finish college," she said quietly.

"You didn't?" Brandt cast a puzzled glance in Walter's direction. "But I thought we agreed—"

"Look at the letter of recommendation she brought with her. I don't think you'll quibble about technicalities, Brandt."

Meredith handed over the long white envelope, and Brandt scanned the contents, his brow furrowed. "Very impressive," he murmured.

"I know I'm capable of doing the work, Mr. Dahlberg."

"Are you sure?" he returned. "Most of the people I've interviewed so far seem to think I'm looking for some sort of glorified secretary. I'm not. The clerical department takes care of all my needs in that area. What I want is someone with a background in mathematics who is capable of intense concentration and painstaking attention to detail. There are times when I have to make important decisions based on my assistant's interpretation of test data. Often even a minor error can be critical. I can't afford carelessness."

"I'm never careless," Meredith stated flatly.

"Oh, really?" Brandt drawled. "You can still say that after that incident in the parking lot?" He'd meant the remark as a joke, but Meredith's expression indicated she was not amused.

He raised his hands in defeat and with a winsome grin placated her. "Relax, please. I've decided you're right— maybe it would be a good idea to have some kind of sign at that crossing. I'll ask maintenance to look into it."

"I'm sure your employees will be grateful."

Brandt stared at her. "Despite all that fiery hair, you're a cool one, aren't you?" She returned his gaze blandly. After a moment he continued. "You're obviously a woman of strong opinions. How do you feel about hard work and dedication? One reason I tend to prefer people with college degrees is that at least they've demonstrated they're capable of setting a goal and fulfilling it. I can't overemphasize how important it is that my assistant be prepared to devote a tremendous amount of time and energy to this job, and to keep on doing so. The last person who worked for me was adequate in the beginning, but after he became interested in that religious order he eventually joined, he wasn't worth a damn. To top it all, he took off without notice, leaving me in the lurch—"

Walter, who had been listening to the interview in puzzled silence, barked with laughter. "Oh, come on now, Brandt, the guy was certifiable! Somehow I can't see the young lady here running off to join a cult."

Brandt's mouth twitched into a wry smile as he glanced at his boss. "No, probably not." When he faced Meredith again, his expression was enigmatic. "Ms Forrester, legally I can't ask you about your marital status or whether you plan to have children, but if there's any reason you can't commit yourself to this job for the foreseeable future, then I'd appreciate your being honest with me."

Meredith's response was instantaneous. "I want this job. It's the only thing that matters."

"In that case, I'll give your application serious consideration. Thank you for dropping by."

The interview was at an end. With a sigh Meredith rose again and held out her hand to Walter. "It really was a pleasure to meet you. I hope we see each other again sometime."

"I'll look forward to it, Meredith," he said warmly, catching her fingers in his large paw. "Next time you see that professor of yours, give her my regards and tell her I owe her one."

"I'll do that." Resignedly she glanced at Brandt. "Mr. Dahlberg, I appreciate your taking a few moments—"

He wasn't listening. "Meredith Forrester," he repeated, his fair brows knit with the effort to remember. "Why does that name seem so familiar?"

Meredith fled before he could answer his own question.

Too keyed up to go home for lunch, she decided to grab a hamburger somewhere, then do some grocery shopping to take advantage of her day off from bookkeeping. During the past few days, she and her brother, excited by their respective appointments, had thought little about food; the apartment's larder was almost empty.

She was just unloading the last overstuffed sack from the back of the van, praying the paper would not rip and scatter oranges all over the oily floor of the carport, when her Toyota zoomed into the parking area. Tires squealed as Mike wheeled into the vacant space beside the van, jamming on the brakes barely in time to avoid hitting the back wall of the garage. Meredith cringed. Considering what had happened to their parents, she'd never been able to understand her brother's cavalier attitude toward driving.

Their parents had been itinerant musicians, lovable but irresponsible. Living like gypsies, they dragged their children with them from one engagement to the next, one town after another. In the era of vaudeville, Meredith would have been described as having been born in a trunk. As it happened, her birth certificate indicated she'd been born in a hospital in South Carolina, but the family had left the state long before she was old enough to form any impressions of it.

Her earliest memory was of perching on a wobbly stool between her banjo-strumming father and her beautiful flame-haired mother, who played the clarinet. In front of them Mike beat time with a tambourine while his baby sister piped out the old torch song, "St. Louis Woman," for the indifferent patrons of a Wisconsin pizza parlor.

Wisconsin had been followed by Indiana, and then Ohio, or maybe it was Illinois. Meredith couldn't remember, just as she could no longer recollect the succession of cramped apartments and seedy motels in which they'd lived. According to Mike, once or twice when jobs were scarce the family had camped out in their old wood-sided station wagon, but Meredith couldn't remember that, either.

She did know that this peripatetic life-style had allowed her and her brother no friends, no opportunity to grow close to anyone but each other. Everything and everyone else was a dizzy blur, passing like the fence posts she used to count for amusement through the car window.

Another thing Meredith recalled clearly was the music—brassy Dixieland jazz that always sounded so cheery or its soulful, rending sister style, the blues. She had learned to sing the blues at a very early age.

As her brother had, Meredith performed from the time she could walk. For a long time she assumed all children lived as they did, regularly confronting crowds of adult strangers who might be enthusiastic or bored or even abusive. When she grew old enough to realize that there was another, normal way of life, she had begged her parents to let her drop out of the act.

Deeply hurt, her mother and father had reminded her the Forresters were a family act, they were always going to work together. Someday, God willing, they would get their big break together. Because her adored big brother accepted his parents' dream wholeheartedly, Meredith decided she must be hateful and selfish to want to break away from her family. She did not complain again.

Ironically, it was she who became the star of their little quartet. Like their parents, Mike was a good but not outstanding musician with a natural flair for most instruments. By some quirk of biology Meredith's voice matured early into a ripe, full-bodied mezzo that was startling when it poured from her little-girl throat.

Bookings increased when the senior Forresters began to feature Meredith as the focus of the act. Singing songs she was far too young to understand, she learned lyrics by rote. While Meredith did enjoy singing, she hated being in the limelight. Increasingly self-conscious about her carrot-red hair and freckles, she felt like a freak. More than ever she longed to settle down and live the way other kids did.

It took a tragedy to make her wish come true. Late one spring when she was thirteen, the family drove to northern California to attend the Dixieland Jubilee in Sacramento, a newly organized annual jazz festival that was already acquiring an international reputation. Afterward, Meredith's mother and father judged that with the numerous clubs and military bases in the region, they ought to be able to find enough bookings to support the family for a few months. They decided to stay put for the summer. Three weeks later, one of the station wagon's bald tires blew out on a freeway, sending the car careening into a bridge abutment. Both parents were killed instantly.

Bringing her thoughts back to the present, Meredith greeted her brother with forced brightness. "You're back early. How was San Francisco?"

Mike stepped out of the car, and hunched his shoulders stiffly, shaking his head. He was a small man, only a couple of inches taller than Meredith, but he was striking. He had inherited their father's almost-black hair and their mother's flawless white skin—a porcelain complexion

Meredith had always coveted. The combination gave him the intense, romantic look of a poet. Not all the girls who attended performances of his band, the New Helvetia Jazz Society, did so because they were fans of Dixieland music.

When Mike didn't answer right away, Meredith probed carefully. "I assumed you'd stay in the city till this evening. I thought you might want to check out what groups were playing."

"No. I just wanted to get home."

The laconic reply worried Meredith. "What's the matter? Something happened, I can tell. Did the people at the ad agency change their minds about that tape you sent them? I thought the reason they called you for the interview in the first place was because they liked your material."

"Oh, they liked the material, all right." He did not elaborate. After a moment his expression cleared slightly, and he noticed the laden bags in Meredith's arms. "Oh, hell, it was my turn to do the grocery shopping, wasn't it, Merry? I'm sorry. Here, let me carry those for you." Relieving Meredith of her load, he strode out of the carport and headed along the concrete path leading to their apartment.

Watching him go, Meredith sighed. Something was bothering her brother, and all her sisterly instincts clamored to ferret out the trouble and safeguard him from it. She felt very protective of Mike. She supposed her custodial attitude was ironic, given that he was five years her senior and had practically raised her. But somehow their roles in the relationship had reversed the night she discovered him drunk and sobbing among the ruins of his record collection.

Until that moment she hadn't realized the great strength
she derived from knowing what she wanted out of life. Her
brother might be baffled by her interest in a subject he
found as boring as applied mathematics, but at least Meredith had always been confident that once she completed
her education she'd be able to establish a career in her
chosen field. But Mike's ambitions were more elusive, he
was determined to be a star . . . whatever that meant.

Meredith realized how much he must be haunted by the
example of their parents, two equally determined people
who had gone to their deaths with that same brass ring still
just beyond their grasp. For their sakes as well as for Mike,
she vowed once more to do everything possible to help her
brother achieve his goal.

Scurrying after him along the walk, she demanded, "So
what happened in San Francisco? Tell me all about it."

Mike halted at the front door of their apartment where
the rest of the grocery sacks were piled on the steps, waiting to be carried inside. "Not now, hon," he said, turning
to smile gently as he pushed open the door. "I'm still sort-
ing things out in my head. Besides, we have just about
enough time to put all this food away before we get ready
for the gig tonight."

"Gig?" Meredith echoed, grimacing in dismay. "You
didn't tell me there was supposed to be a performance this
evening."

"Of course I did. At least, I thought I did. Jack Barnes
at Sonora Sue's called yesterday. The act they booked fell
through, and Jack wanted to know if we could fill in. Since
we were free tonight, I said sure."

"Well, as long as the guys don't mind the short notice,"
Meredith murmured with a shrug. She began to stack cans
in the kitchen cupboard. All at once she froze, her hand

in midair. "Mike," she said carefully, "I do hope you weren't expecting me to do vocals...."

"Jack asked for you specifically."

Meredith shivered. "Damn it, Mike, you can't just spring something like that on me without warning! I can't sing tonight. I haven't rehearsed for days. I'm tired and all I want to do is relax and watch TV. Besides, my white dress is at the cleaners."

"So wear the blue one you bought for the festival."

"I haven't altered it yet."

"Wear it anyway!" Mike retorted impatiently. "Nobody's going to notice if it's a little tight. You're not exactly Dolly Parton, you know!" When Meredith bristled, her brother quickly changed his tack. "Good grief, sis, don't worry about the stupid dress. You'll look beautiful no matter how it fits. As for your singing, you know as well as I do that a few scales are all it'll take to warm up those pipes of yours." His complacent chuckle faded as he added seriously, "In any case, when Jack asked us to fill in, I could hardly say no. After all he's done for us, convincing the Jubilee committee to finally give the band a spot on the program..."

Sighing resignedly, Meredith dropped the subject. Although performing in a noisy saloon was absolutely the last thing she felt like doing that evening, she knew she couldn't turn down a request from a man who'd helped make one of her brother's most cherished dreams come true. For the first time ever, thanks to Jack, Mike's band was going to participate in the annual Dixieland Jubilee.

In the years since Meredith and her family had drifted into Sacramento, the Jubilee had grown into a huge music festival known to jazz buffs all over the world. Each Memorial Day weekend, attendance topped the hundred-thousand mark. Groups from as far away as Europe and

Australia clamored for spots in the program. To be invited to appear even as a warm-up act in some out-of-the-way cabaret was a great compliment.

Meredith was delighted for her brother and the other five men who comprised the New Helvetia Jazz Society. Except for Mike, each of them had an outside job, ranging from plumber to librarian. For the other members the band was strictly an avocation, but they were all dedicated musicians, devoting long hours to their playing. It was gratifying to see their hard work appreciated.

Besides, she reasoned, if the exposure and connections the band made at the Jubilee would help Mike find the success he craved, perhaps then Meredith would be free at last to concentrate on her own ambitions. For that, she'd squeeze into the stupid dress somehow.

Shoving a box of cornflakes into Mike's hand, Meredith ordered, "Well, brother dear, if you expect me to sing tonight, I'm going to have to practice awhile. So why don't you finish putting away the groceries? Some coffee would be nice, too."

Without waiting for a reply, she disappeared into the living room where an old upright piano—disreputable looking but perfectly tuned—occupied most of one wall. Atop it was propped a large wooden placard with Gothic lettering that announced The New Helvetia Jazz Society, with Merry Forrest. The sign teetered as she pulled out the bench and sat down. With a sigh of resignation, Meredith struck a C-major chord and began to sing scales.

SHE WAS SEATED beside Mike in the van, blinking hard as her eyes slowly adjusted to the contact lenses she wore for performances. It occurred to her then that not once during the afternoon had her brother bothered to ask how her own interview had gone.

Surely she ought to be used to his self-absorption by now, Meredith reminded herself. Their parents had been equally deaf to anything but their music. Still, his disinterest hurt.

She began to toy with the fringes of her blue silk flapper dress, a genuine antique she'd discovered in a used-clothing store. The outfit had been purchased to coordinate with the dashing striped blazers and straw skimmers the men in the band planned to wear for the Jubilee. It fit well everywhere except the bodice, where the low neckline had been cut for the flat-chested look of the twenties, making Meredith's modest bustline seem buxom.

As they neared their destination, Meredith wished she hadn't allowed her brother to talk her into wearing the dress before she had an opportunity to alter it. The tight fit made her feel uncomfortable and conspicuous, as if she were being deliberately provocative. She had a shawl to wear, but she still hoped she wouldn't pop a seam while she was singing.

Brushing her long hair until it glowed like embers pouring over her shoulders, she returned her hairbrush to her purse and leaned back in her seat, trying to relax. She swayed as the vehicle passed beneath a triple-decked freeway overpass. The music stands in the rear of the van bounced when the panel truck rounded a corner and hit cobbled pavement. "Slow down, Mike," she insisted.

They were driving through the narrow, crowded streets of Old Sacramento. The riverfront portion of the city had been restored to look as it had during the gold rush when sailing ships from all over the world had carried fortyniners, lured to California by the promise of instant riches. A hundred years later, a massive reclamation project at the confluence of the Sacramento and American Rivers had turned the area into the town's most popular tourist attraction, home of Victorian-flavored shops and restaurants, the California State Railroad Museum, and the Dixieland Jubilee.

As the gas streetlights flickered on, Mike turned the van into an alley. Meredith, peering into the twilight, noticed a strolling couple who emerged suddenly out of the shadows of the covered plank sidewalk. "For heaven's sake, watch out for pedestrians!" she squealed.

"They were a mile away," Mike retorted, shooting her an irritated frown. "And don't squint, you'll spoil your makeup."

Meredith's temper flared. "Damn it, if you don't quit sniping at me, I'm going to get out of this van right now and go home!"

Her brother recoiled, staring. "You're in a lousy mood tonight, Merry! You've been bitchy ever since this afternoon."

"I feel bitchy. I told you I didn't want to sing."

"Well, I hope you'll keep those feelings to yourself. There's Jack waiting with the rest of the guys." He nodded toward six men clustered in the alley by the rear entrance to Sonora Sue's Saloon. "They're all depending on you."

"Yeah, I know," Meredith muttered.

Shaking his head, Mike patted her hand consolingly. "Look, hon, I'm sorry I barked. I guess I'm just getting jumpy, with the jazz festival so close. Everyone's on edge these days . . . even you. So what I want you to do is forget about the Jubilee tonight and just relax. You know singing helps you unwind."

Meredith regarded Mike skeptically; his face was grave with loving concern. "Whatever you say," she murmured.

To her surprise, she discovered her brother was right—at least at first. The two numbers the band opened with

were instrumentals, and as she sat in a chair next to the pianist, hands folded sedately in her lap, her mouth curved
into the vanilla-bland stage smile she had learned to cul-
tivate when she was a toddler. She felt her tension ease.
She did love music. The traditional jazz she'd been raised
with was part of her lifeblood. It just wasn't her whole life.

The guys sounded good tonight. Their excitement over
the forthcoming Jubilee showed in their playing, and their
enthusiasm was infectious. When Mike and the trombone player pealed out the brassy opening of "South
Rampart Street Parade," the fanfare was punctuated by the
drummer. The notes echoed and reverberated off the walls
of the smoky cabaret. Patrons who had ignored the musicians while they warmed up suddenly lifted their heads
from their drinks and grinned with pleasure. When clarinet, piano and banjo joined in, conversation stopped. By
the time the selection reached its raucous, rousing conclusion, half the people in the audience were clapping with
the beat.

The second number featured a pyrotechnical banjo solo
that elicited enthusiastic applause, then it was time for a
change of pace and Meredith's first vocal—a new arrangement Mike had written for an old standard. Clapping and whistles greeted her as she tossed her shawl
rakishly around her shoulders. It was a teasing, apparently alluring maneuver that draped the stole over the too-
tight bodice of her dress. She stepped to the microphone.
Ruffling her hair, she flashed a glowing smile and surveyed the dim room, searching for a friendly face on which
to focus while she sang. It was a trick her parents had
taught her when she was a little girl, a way of appearing
to relate to the audience while in fact all her concentration was on the music. She almost never really saw the

faces she stared at; with her contact lenses, everything was blurry beyond the tables nearest the stage.

As the pianist played the pickup to Meredith's entrance, her hazel eyes locked on a smear of light toward the back of the room—some man with fair hair. The color reminded her of the way the sun had played on Brandt Dahlberg's tumbled locks in the parking lot that morning. He'd certainly been a pleasure to look at. She wondered if her disappointment over the job at Warcom was solely because she'd wanted to work there. Beaming in the direction of the man at the far table, Meredith began her song.

"You got your eye on someone?" Mike murmured curiously, when later the band took a break.

He and Meredith were leaning against the wall in a darkened hall behind the stage, sharing sandwiches and beer. The other musicians had taken their refreshments and wandered away. Meredith noticed that Don, the clarinet player and the only unmarried band member besides Mike, was chatting up a couple of girls, one of whom looked too young to be in a bar.

"I always thought you were above coming on to men in the audience, but from the way you kept staring at that guy in the back row, I thought you might be interested."

Meredith rubbed away the lines of fatigue that creased her forehead. Unlike her brother, who found performances exhilarating, she always felt drained after she sang. "I couldn't see him well enough to tell whether I'm interested or not," she bantered. "Is he cute?"

Shrugging, Mike conceded, "I guess he's all right, if you go for the beachboy type. Not only that, he appeared to be alone. From the way he was scowling at you, though, I suspect you'd have your work cut out warming him up. He seemed angry about something."

"Maybe he just doesn't like my voice."

"If he doesn't, he's a jerk! You're sounding good tonight, Merry. Keep it up, and before you know it, we'll all be rich and famous!"

Meredith grimaced. "I'll do my best."

"Of course, you will. You always do."

Despite her brother's confidence, as the evening dragged on Meredith became increasingly doubtful that she was doing her best for him or anyone else. The closed room was hot, making her long to abandon the shawl; the air was stuffy with cigarette smoke that stung her eyes and distracted her from the music.

When her concentration wavered, the depression she had pushed aside earlier returned to plague her. Refusing to look in the direction of the man she'd noticed earlier, Meredith kept her gaze trained firmly on the people nearest the stage. At one table sat the two girls who had been talking to the clarinetist. The younger, a petite brunette wearing too much eye shadow, gazed soulfully at Mike.

At last the set ended with a loud, driving rendition of "Alabammy Bound," another of Mike's new arrangements. As soon as the applause faded and the band began to break up, Meredith tossed her wrap onto a chair and fled to the rest room to remove her contacts. When she emerged again, blinking with relief behind the wide-lensed glasses she'd been carrying in her handbag, she ran directly into the hard wall of Brandt Dahlberg's chest.

"You!" she choked in dismay, steadying herself. In the dim light of the hallway his eyes were dark, crinkled with laugh lines, but there was no laughter to match the wary smile on his lips. "What are you doing here?" Meredith demanded.

"Really, Ms Forrester, do you think you're the only jazz buff in Sacramento? I've been coming to Sonora Sue's for years to listen to the music. In fact, I think I've seen you perform here before."

"Oh," Meredith floundered. "I—I didn't realize . . ."

His voice deepened. "But if you mean why am I here in this hallway," he continued deliberately, "surely you must have expected me to follow up on that rather blatant invitation you've been telegraphing in my direction all evening?"

Meredith gasped and shook her head in protest. "But I didn't! I mean, I didn't know who it was." She felt herself begin to blush as she realized how that remark sounded. Quickly she amended, "I mean, it may have looked like I was smiling at you, but I really couldn't see. My contact lenses...I wear them when I perform, but they don't work very well."

"Then why wear them at all? If Ella Fitzgerald can wear glasses when she sings, why can't you?"

"Because I'm not Ella Fitzgerald and never will be," Meredith sighed. "Anyway, the band insists."

Brandt's brows shot up. "I'd think you'd have enough gumption to tell the whole band to take a flying leap."

"I wish..." Meredith lapsed into rueful silence and gazed mutely at Brandt. He was even more handsome in casual clothes than he'd been in his business suit, she decided objectively, a little surprised by the observation. She'd always been partial to gray flannel, but on Brandt sportswear seemed much more comfortable, more fitting somehow.

A knit shirt open at the throat stretched across his broad shoulders and exposed the golden skin at his throat. Tight, faded jeans displayed his muscular thighs in a way that was even more erotic than the brief cycling shorts he'd worn that morning had been. Meredith felt her body react hungrily.

With affected nonchalance she noted, "I'm not sure I would have recognized you even if I had been wearing my glasses. You—you don't look the same."

"Neither do you."

Wiping her damp palms on the silk dress, Meredith muttered uncomfortably, "These are just my working clothes."

"I thought that prim little beige outfit you wore this morning was supposed to be your working clothes," Brandt countered. "That's one of the reasons it took me so long to recall where I'd seen you before. Not that a gorgeous redhead with a sultry voice is easy to forget, but you have to remember that Meredith Forrester, dedicated mathematician, seems very far removed from Merry Forrest, torch singer."

His eyes dropped, and Meredith's blush darkened. She could feel scalding color drip down her throat to her chest, where her rounded breasts swelled provocatively over the low neckline of the flapper dress, forming a deep V. She was sure every freckle on her body must be aglow. She stared up at him, trying to decipher his expression.

"I like your outfit, Merry Forrest," he murmured.

Meredith licked her lips. "D-don't call me Merry," she stammered huskily. "Nobody calls me Merry except my family. It's just a s-stage name."

"Funny that you didn't mention the stage on your resumé."

"Why should I? Singing is just a hobby. It isn't germane."

"It isn't—as long as you do it strictly in your spare time. I cannot permit outside interests to interfere with your work for me. I've already had one assistant leave me stranded, and I don't want it to happen again. Besides, I

know how seductive a show business career can seem to
a young woman—"

"I thought your assistant was a man who joined some
cult," Meredith broke in.

"He was," Brandt replied. "I was talking about—" He
broke off and shaped his mouth into a reassuring smile.
"Forget it. I just want to be sure that, should it become
necessary, you'd be willing to give up all this to work for
me. I can't emphasize strongly enough that whoever I hire
as my assistant will have to be willing to commit all her
time and energy—"

"Are you telling me I've got the job?" Meredith's eyes
widened joyfully.

"I'm telling you I'm willing to take you on a probation-
ary basis. After you left, Walter convinced me to give you
a try despite your lack of experience or credentials. He
liked you on sight, and he has complete faith in the judgment of that professor friend of his who wrote the letter
of recommendation."

"That's very kind of him. I'll have to be sure to thank
him."

Brandt shrugged. "Well, as Walter reminded me rather
pointedly, if he were applying for a job at Warcom today,
he'd have trouble qualifying because he doesn't have a
college degree either!"

Meredith grinned at the memory of the big man with the
beard. "I'll have to work hard to justify his faith in me."

"You'll do better to prove yourself to me," Brandt reminded her. "Walter may have talked me into giving you
a shot at this job, but the ultimate decision as to whether
you keep it is mine. I'll be frank. At this point I'm skeptical not only about your qualifications but about your
dedication. Although you may have some natural flair for
math, I find it impossible to believe that a woman as tal-

ented and beautiful as you is going to be content for long, working with statistics and equations."

Meredith bridled, angered rather than flattered by his remark. Lifting her chin, she repeated, "A woman, Mr. Dahlberg? You'd better be careful, that sounds almost actionable."

"You mean you'd sue me for sex discrimination if you thought you could make a case?"

"Damn right I would, if that's what it takes to prove I'm serious about this job. I'm not going to let anyone stop me from getting what I want out of life."

Brandt nodded. "Well and good, but sometimes that's easier said than done...." His gaze moved leisurely down her body, noting every swell and indentation where the blue silk clung. Meredith surveyed him with equal candor. When their eyes flicked upward to meet squarely, the awareness that sparked between them was almost visible in the dim hallway.

Someone brushed past them in the corridor, and with an effort Meredith composed herself. She heard Jack Barnes, the manager of Sonora Sue's, declare, "You and the guys were really great tonight, Meredith! Thanks for filling in on such short notice."

"Any time, Jack," she responded absently. "Thanks for asking us." Her face became a cordial, composed mask as she looked at Brandt again. "And thank you for giving me the job at Warcom, Mr. Dahlberg. I promise you won't regret it."

"We'll see." Taking a deep breath, he reached up and brushed back a strand of flaming hair that had fallen across her cheek. His fingertips were slightly rough, dragging with tender abrasion across her skin. "You're going

to be an interesting woman to work with, Merry Forrest,"
he murmured. "I'll see you Monday."

With a brisk nod he turned on his heel and disappeared
back into the main room of the saloon.

3

"HEY, MERRY." Mike interrupted her reverie as she stared in the direction Brandt had disappeared. "C'mon, sis, wake up!"

"I am awake."

"You look like you're in a daze or something."

Pushing herself away from the wall, Meredith twisted her neck to ease the cramped muscles. Until that moment she hadn't realized just how very tense she'd been during the encounter with her new employer. She wondered if daily contact with Brandt Dahlberg would dampen the dangerous effect he had on her senses—the effect they seemed to have on each other. She hoped so. Flattering as it was to know he was also attracted to her, she didn't want that interfering with her work. She was serious about this job.

"You're drifting off again," Mike muttered.

With a tired grin Meredith conceded, "I guess I am. It's been a long, weird day. The instant we get back to the apartment, I intend to fall into bed and stay there till Sunday. Do you think you'll have the van loaded and ready to leave soon?"

Suddenly Mike looked uncomfortable. Diffidently he began, "Merry, hon, I need to talk to you about that."

"If you're planning to ask me to drive your blasted van home, you can forget it. Once today was enough. You know I hate that thing."

"Actually, I was going to ask if you'd mind taking a taxi."
When Meredith's eyes widened in astonishment, he added
hastily, "Oh, I'll pay for it, if that's what's bothering you."

All at once she was completely alert, her fatigue forgotten. "What's going on? Why on earth would I need a
taxi?"

Her brother shifted restlessly, a shy, oddly boyish
expression softening his features. "Well, Don and I met
these girls, and—"

"And you don't want to waste time driving your sister
home." Glancing over her shoulder into the main room,
Meredith spotted the clarinetist talking earnestly to the
pair of young women she'd noticed earlier. She frowned.
Both girls appeared presentable and attractive, and since
their matching T-shirts were the kind available only to
volunteers who actually worked during the Dixieland Jubilee, she guessed they must be serious jazz fans, not
groupies. But Meredith was also sure that beneath her
dramatic makeup one of them, a short brunette with frizzy
permed curls, was a teenager. She'd be willing to bet
money that the ID the girl used to get into Sonora Sue's
was borrowed or faked.

Carefully she observed, "Cute kids, but they're a little
young for you and Don, don't you think, Mike?"

He shrugged. "Not really. Cheryl, the one with brown
hair, told us they're both twenty-two and they're seniors
at Sac State."

Meredith snorted. "Honestly, I had no idea you were so
gullible! Regardless of what Sherry or Cheryl or whoever
she is told you, her friend may be twenty-two, but *she*
looks like jailbait."

"Meredith!" When her brother unexpectedly spit out her
full name, she regarded him curiously. His hazel eyes, so

like her own, were dark and affronted. "Back off, Merry," he warned in low, clipped tones. "Just . . . back off."

"Of course. Sorry." Aware she had overstepped one of the invisible barriers between her and Mike, she retreated. The two of them never questioned each other about their love lives. The tacit agreement was one way they avoided the possessiveness, even jealousy, that were otherwise almost inevitable between two people who had been dependent on each other since they were little more than children.

Meredith had always known there were women in her brother's life occasionally, but except for a nagging concern that it was because of her that he hadn't married one of them long ago, she did not think about them. Mike in turn respected her privacy. When she turned sixteen, he had bashfully handed her a pamphlet on birth control, but he had never asked whether she had read it. Both knew the other would always be there if needed, and that knowledge, plus their innate common sense, had carried them into adulthood relatively unscathed.

Meredith glanced at the two girls again, then at her brother. From the rapt expression on his face, she could tell he was strongly attracted to the brunette. She sighed. Maybe the girl really was older than she looked. In any case, Mike wasn't stupid.

With a fond smile, Meredith said, "Don't worry about the taxi; I'll ask if one of the other guys can give me a lift. You and Don have a good time with your dates. Just be careful, okay?"

"Okay." Mike relaxed. Giving her arm an awkward pat, he headed down the hall. "Thanks, hon," he called back over his shoulder, "I'll see you . . . when I see you. Don't wait up."

"I won't. Good night." Meredith wondered why she suddenly felt so forlorn.

The banjo player told Meredith he was meeting his wife and another couple for a late supper at a restaurant near the Railroad Museum, but the drummer said he'd be happy to drive her back to the apartment if she didn't mind waiting half an hour or so before they left. Although she was anxious to go home, Meredith thanked him for his offer with as good grace as she could muster; it wasn't his fault her brother had left her stranded. In the meantime, however, she needed some fresh air.

When she stepped onto the plank sidewalk in front of Sonora Sue's, the change from the club's stuffy over-heated atmosphere to the balmy darkness outside was sharp enough to make her grateful for her shawl, which she wrapped around her shivering shoulders. She re-minded herself she ought to enjoy the spring coolness while it lasted; by the time the festival rolled around on the last weekend in May temperatures could easily soar to ninety or one hundred degrees.

The building in which Sonora Sue's was located faced directly onto the Embarcadero, a wide cobbled street following the reinforced east bank of the Sacramento River. Moving out of the path of couples strolling along the plank sidewalk, Meredith huddled back in the shadows. The river was running high because of snowmelt from the Sierra Nevada, and beneath the laughter of passing strangers she could hear the scud of water against levee stones behind the flood control wall. Such a troubled sound, agitated and morose. It made her restless just to listen to it. She wondered if it was her fatigue that de-pressed her, or maybe she was still unsettled by that puz-zling encounter with Brandt Dahlberg. Or perhaps she felt lonely because it was Friday night and her brother, her

friends, everyone else in the world seemed to be in pairs
except her.

Days are lonesome, nights are so long. Wistfully she
hummed the refrain of her favorite Bessie Smith recording, classic blues performed with an artistry that never
failed to stagger Meredith. She loved the song. She just
wished the words didn't seem quite so apt at the moment.

She'd been alone for a long time. Her history professor
had been exactly that—history—well before she dropped
out of college, and after they'd parted by mutual consent
there had been no one else. Sometimes Meredith thought
she might be more comfortable if only she could live like
her brother, taking love where she found it. But although
she enjoyed sex, she disliked casual sex. Picking up men
in bars was not her style.

The piercing toot of a boat horn interrupted her mus-
ing, and Meredith looked up with a start. Half a mile
downstream a drawbridge with two tall towers spanned
the river, and as she stared, lights began to flash and bells
rang, the dissonant clang echoing along the riverbanks.
The center section of the bridge was about to be raised for
some passing vessel. Meredith smiled; watching the spans
go up and down was a rare treat. Although Sacramento
waterways were full of pleasure boats, most were small
enough to pass easily beneath the bridges. Through the
lace of iron fretwork she spotted a single red light waver-
ing high over the water as it approached the bridge from
the opposite side. She guessed the beacon was topping the
mast of a large sailboat trolling upriver under power. She
decided to cross the road for a better view.

Intent on reaching the floodwall in time to see the boat
pass under the bridge, she scurried across the Embarcadero, dodging parked cars, her eyes trained on her feet to
make sure her high heels did not cause her to stumble on

the rough cobbles. She failed to notice that she was moving away from the light, into an isolated area full of nooks and shadows. At the wall, when she stretched on tiptoe to see over the top she failed to notice the dark figure crouched nearby.

"Need some help, lady?" a slurred voice cackled roughly, almost at her shoulder. Meredith's heart lurched, and she jerked around. Out of the gloom rose a cadaverously thin man with a tobacco-stained beard. He seemed to be wearing at least three ragged shirts, one on top of the other. All reeked of alcohol.

"No, thank you," she said stiffly, her throat chalky with fright. She cursed herself for stupidly forgetting the transients who sometimes lurked along the riverfront. "I'll just be going." Mentally she evaluated her chances of escape. The wall was at her back, the concrete clammy against her bare shoulders, and her heels were slipping on the uneven pavement. Running didn't seem a viable option.

The derelict shuffled closer, kicking aside an empty bottle wrapped in a brown paper bag. Meredith tensed. "Aw, what's the hurry, sweetie?" the man wheedled with a grin. His teeth were brown. "You wanna watch the boats? We'll watch 'em together. I can tell you all about boats. I used to be a sailor before I got down on my luck. You wouldn't have a dollar for an old sailor, would you? How's about a cigarette?" He noticed the silk fringes on her costume. "Hey, that's a pretty dress. I like them tassly things." Dirty hands stretched toward her.

With a guttural squeal Meredith exploded. Batting the man's arms away, she curled her nails and spit, "Lay one finger on me and I'll rip your throat out!"

The man blanched in alarm and jerked back. "I—I was only admiring the dress," he choked, retreating. "I remember when I was a sailor, the girls used to—"

"She's not interested in when you were a sailor." A tall figure loomed out of the shadows, his face set, dangerous. "She's with me."

Meredith relaxed, limp with relief. "Brandt!"

His expression was rueful. "I was very chivalrously dashing to your rescue, but it looks as if you don't need me." He scowled stonily at the derelict, who cringed. "As for you—"

"Sorry, mister, sorry," the man mumbled, shrinking from Brandt's glare. "I was just . . . sorry. No harm intended."

Brandt turned away and, offering Meredith his arm, he muttered, "Let's get out of here." Together they walked back across the Embarcadero.

They did not speak again until he had nudged her into a chair in a dark corner of Sonora Sue's. Signaling for the cocktail waitress, he flopped into the seat beside her. His voice was harsh with concern as he demanded, "Are you all right? Why on earth were you wandering around alone in the dark, especially dressed the way you are? I thought you left an hour ago."

"I was killing time till one of the guys in the band could give me a lift home," Meredith explained miserably, still shaken by the encounter with the derelict. Glancing around, she did not spot the drummer. "I don't know where my friend is now." Acutely aware of curious eyes watching from other tables, she pulled her shawl protectively around her hunched shoulders. "While I was waiting, I decided to watch the drawbridge. I just didn't think."

"I'll say," Brandt admonished. "You're lucky you didn't get hurt. I don't mean by that feeble old wino—you seemed to be handling him just fine by yourself when I came along—but a lot of bums on the street these days are young and mean, you know. . . ."

"Yes, I do know. I've been brushing off drunks since I was thirteen, but it never pays to be careless." She shivered. "If you hadn't come along . . . I'm very grateful for your help. Thank you."

"Forget it," he said laconically. "It's all over now."

When the waitress reappeared with the drinks Brandt had ordered, Meredith tasted the whiskey dubiously, made a face, and set down her glass. "I hate Scotch," she declared.

"I'm sorry . . . I'll order wine, if you prefer. I just thought you could use something to relax you," Brandt said.

His obvious worry rallied Meredith's spirits. "This'll do," she said sipping her drink. She smiled. There was something very pleasant about having a man fuss over her.

"When you're finished, I'll take you home," he offered.

Meredith looked at him in mock surprise. "Oh, really? Do you think we'll both fit on your ten-speed?"

Brandt threw back his head and laughed, a rich, happy laugh, full of charm and good humor. Meredith found the sound very attractive, almost as attractive as the crinkles that formed around his eyes or the deep dimples that bracketed his wide smile when he beamed at her.

I could fall in love with this man, she thought, astonished. She wondered if her amazement showed in her face.

The instant Brandt's gaze met hers, his expression sobered, his eyes grew hooded and intent. "You're feeling better," he said, his voice barely audible over the noise of the nightclub. "That's good. I'm glad you've gotten over your scare."

She moved nearer to hear him, until their elbows touched and she could feel the heat of his thigh next to hers. "I deserved to be scared, for being so stupid. I'm glad you were there."

"Always delighted to be of service to a lady." His glance flicked down to the swell of her bosom beneath the too-tight dress. He took a deep breath and laid his palm over hers. She could feel ridges of callus along the undersides of his fingers, where his curled hand would clench the handlebars of a bicycle. The hardened skin was just rough enough to tease her softer flesh.

"Meredith," he asked slowly, deliberately, his dark tones lengthening the name into a caress, "I brought my car tonight. Would you like me to take you home now?"

She didn't have to ponder her answer. Lacing her fingers through his, she whispered, "Yes, Brandt, I'd like that very much."

As HE GUIDED his Volvo along the dark streets canopied with poplar and magnolia trees, Brandt glanced sidelong at Meredith's profile. In the headlights of a passing automobile he could see even white teeth press into her lower lip, chewing off her lipstick, and she was fidgeting with her glasses. "So tell me about Merry Forrest," he suggested breezily.

Meredith met his gaze, her expression quizzical. "What about her?"

Brandt shrugged. "Oh, anything at all. How she got to be a jazz singer. Why she seems almost embarrassed by her talent.... If those questions are too personal, maybe you could explain about the stage name. Meredith Forrester and Merry Forrest are so similar it hardly seems worthwhile to differentiate."

"Would you believe it was an economic decision?" Meredith responded lightly. "I don't know if you noticed the placard at the edge of the stage tonight—*The New Helvetia Jazz Society, with Merry Forrest*—but my brother had it painted a couple of years ago. He was really short of money at the time, and the calligrapher charged by the letter. So Mike figured he could save a few bucks by using my family nickname."

"But if money was that critical, instead of just truncating Forrester, why didn't you change it to something completely different like, oh, maybe Wood? You know, forester, forest, wood?" Brandt grinned. "No, on second thought, Merry Wood sounds like something out of a Robin Hood movie."

Meredith stared. "Brandt," she exclaimed, stunned that he had managed to dredge up one of her most painful memories, "you must be psychic."

"What do you mean?"

Trying not to wince, she explained, "When I was a little girl, things weren't going well—as usual—so my parents got the bright idea of revamping the act and changing the name. Although I've never been able to figure out what connection Robin Hood had with the kind of music we played, for some reason they decided on 'The Woodsmen and Maid Merry.' Mom bought yards and yards of kelly-green cloth—it must have been on sale—and she rented a sewing machine to use in the motel room. Then, while Dad worked on new arrangements, she stitched up costumes for all of us. The two of them settled for new shirts, but my outfit was a short tunic and tights and a felt hat with a feather in it."

"Cute," Brandt commented doubtfully.

Meredith grimaced. "Actually, in that getup, with my red hair and freckles and wing-tipped glasses, I must have looked like a sick elf. But I was only a little girl so I could get away with it. Unfortunately, Mother made a matching costume for my brother."

"Your brother?"

"You know, Mike, the lead horn player in the band. You saw him tonight."

Brandt nodded, surprised. "The guy with dark hair is your brother? The two of you don't look much alike." He frowned thoughtfully. "I had no idea you'd been performing so long. I guess that explains why you sing as well as you do."

"Mike and I have been on the road since we were kids," Meredith explained. "When this stupid episode with the Robin Hood suits took place, I was eight and he was thirteen. He was skinny and small for his age, but he was old enough to know what he looked like."

She shook her head sadly. "Our debut in those costumes was the only time I ever saw Mike balk at performing. We were at a rundown roadhouse someplace in Pennsylvania, steel-working country. There was a little platform stage, no curtains or anything, and Mom and Dad literally had to drag my brother up onto it. I was supposed to follow on cue, singing 'You're Drivin' Me Crazy.' But the instant Mike was shoved into the spotlight, some guy at the bar yelled, 'Hey, kid, who ya s'posed to be, Peter Pan—or are you Tinkerbell?' Then somebody else noticed me and bellowed, 'No, she's Tinkerbell! Can't you see all the spots where the fairy dust hit her?'"

The white Volvo swerved, as if the steering wheel had jerked. "What happened then?"

Meredith sighed. "Mom cued me and I sang. Even in the boondocks, the show must go on." She nodded toward the intersection they were approaching. "Turn left there, please. My place is in the next block."

Brandt was quiet while Meredith unlocked her front door and flicked on the light. When she stepped inside, he followed, dodging the laundry basket full of clean but unsorted laundry that stood in the center of the entry hall.

He glanced through the archway into the living room, noting the single man's shoe that lay abandoned on the rug, the two empty cups on the side table where Meredith dropped her shawl. Shoving his hands deep in the pockets of his jeans, he scowled.

Meredith asked, "What's wrong?"

"You live with someone."

"Just Mike," she explained with a shrug. "He's out for the evening."

Brandt looked at her oddly. "You still live with your brother?"

"Yes. Why? Does it make a difference?"

"No, of course not. But I didn't expect—"

She studied him once again, relishing his lean perfection. It was difficult to believe there wasn't already some other woman touching that athletic body the way she wanted to touch it. Quietly she inquired, "And what about you, Brandt? Any roommates, girlfriends, wives . . ."

He shook his head. "Not at the moment. I had a brief attack of marriage shortly after I went to work for Walter, but it didn't take."

"I'm sorry to hear that."

"Don't be. It was a long time ago."

They fell silent. Meredith gazed at him across the width of the entryway. Inhaling deeply, she could feel the dress pinch her breasts. He was very good to look at, but he was as tense as she was. Beneath his soft knit shirt the muscles of his broad shoulders were corded and bunched. Her eyes grazed his, then darted aside. A wall of restraint seemed to grow higher with each silent second that passed.

Uncomfortably she gestured toward the living room. "Would you like to sit down? I . . . could make some coffee." *Feeble, Meredith, feeble.* She groaned inwardly at the tentative opening.

"Coffee is fine." He seemed as nervous as she was.

Meredith crossed to the love seat and gathered up a stack of sheet music that was scattered on the cushions. "Here, just let me move this mess for you."

Watching her cram the papers into the piano bench, Brandt queried, "Do you play as well as sing?"

"Not really. Mike's the musician of the family. I lack the manual dexterity or fine motor skills or whatever. I can accompany myself on the piano when I'm practicing, but that's about the extent of it." She lowered the lid of the bench and smiled at Brandt. "And how about you? You're a jazz buff. Do you play an instrument?"

"I'm a real virtuoso on the stereo," he replied dryly.

Meredith nodded. "Maybe you'd enjoy looking at our record collection. We have some classics."

Brandt relaxed visibly. Pulling his hands from his pockets, he said, "Thank you. I'd like that."

"Good. The phonograph is over there. Feel free to play anything you want to hear. While you're doing that, I'll put on some coffee and—" She broke off self-consciously. She was *not* going to say she wanted to slip into something more comfortable! Fluffing the delicate silk fringe of her costume, she said, "I really do need to change."

Brandt's eyes darkened as they moved over her body with deliberate slowness. He wet his lips. "You don't have to change a single thing for me," he murmured.

"It would be better if I did." After a moment Brandt nodded in wry agreement.

When Meredith returned to the living room a few moments later, dressed comfortably in jeans and a short-sleeved shirt, she carried two steaming mugs of coffee. Brandt was just setting the stereo's tone arm into the groove on a thick, slightly warped record. From the speakers came a scratchy whooshing noise, but a second later the poor sound was overcome by the mellow tones of a tenor saxophone. Brandt listened raptly.

When Meredith set down the coffee and touched his shoulder, he turned to her and asked, "Where on earth did you find all these 78s? Some of them must be one of a kind. I know you said you had some classics, but I've never even seen an original Coleman Hawkins recording before."

"Mike and I have been collecting for years, and quite a few of them belonged to our folks," Meredith explained. She thought wistfully of the records her brother had broken during that drunken rampage. "There used to be more, but something happened."

"That's too bad. Maybe you ought to consider donating the rest to a museum, before something happens to them, too."

"Maybe."

Once again conversation became desultory, words lagging as the senses spoke louder. Beneath the driving rhythm of the jazz quartet on the phonograph, Meredith was sure she could hear Brandt's breathing and the bass player seemed to mimic the beat of her own heart. She wanted to scream with frustration. She'd never been as aware of a man as she was of Brandt—or as wary.

"Brandt, the coffee's getting cold," she said, trying for normalcy.

He glanced at Meredith, sensing her disquiet. He looked down at the two cups on the table in front of the sofa. All at once his eyes twinkled. Holding out a reassuring hand, he caught her soft fingers in his rough ones and murmured, "Well, in that case, Merry Forrest, I guess we'd better sit down and drink it, shouldn't we?"

He settled onto the cushions, his arm lying along the back of the couch, drawing her down against him so that she fit stiffly into the crook of his arm. "Relax," he whispered, his lips close to her ear.

Meredith looked at him with hesitant eyes. She wondered if he was about to kiss her and suddenly she wasn't sure she was ready for such a move.

Brandt read her expression accurately. Grinning, he stretched across her and picked up her coffee mug, presenting it to her politely. When he picked up his own, Meredith sighed and relaxed.

He was very comfortable to sit with, she mused, closing her eyes as she leaned her head back. The warmth from the coffee cup in her hand was no more pervasive than the heat of his body aligned alongside hers, hip to hip, thigh to thigh. Beneath her nape, she could feel his hard biceps, soothing in its strength. But as she remembered vividly from their first encounter that morning, Brandt was strong all over. Meredith smiled. She liked the way cycling had made his muscles long and smooth, not lumpy. . . .

She swallowed the last of her coffee, and the empty mug was taken from her. Twin clinks indicated he had put away his cup, too. When Brandt settled back against the cushions once more, Meredith could feel his fingers toying with a strand of her bright hair where it spilled over his arm. "So you were a child star?" he queried lightly.

"My parents would have liked me to be," Meredith said, not lifting her lashes. "My mother's deepest regret was that I was the wrong age for the lead in *Annie*. A couple of years' difference and she would have given me a frizzy permanent and decked me out in ugly little dresses with puffed sleeves, completely ignoring the fact that I can't act and have two left feet for dancing!"

"But you can sing, Meredith," Brandt countered, his breath teasing her cheek. "I had no idea how you can sing . . ."

Meredith's eyes popped open. His face was so close to hers that her glasses fogged with each breath. She could see the individual hairs in his mustache, some almost white, others surprisingly red. She wondered if his mouth would feel as hard as the rest of his body. "W-why is it that everyone's so hung up on my singing?" she stammered, moistening her lips with the tip of her tongue. "I was a math major in college, but no one ever remembers that."

"It's a natural reaction," Brandt said. "After all, the only numbers most people enjoy are musical ones."

"Not me. I love working with numbers."

"But why? What do you get from mathematics that you can't get elsewhere?"

Meredith smiled. "Would you believe stability?"

"Stability?" Brandt echoed, staring. "What the hell does that mean?"

Meredith shrugged. "It's simple. When I was a child, we bounced all over the country, never staying in any one place very long. I lost track of how many different schools I attended. One of the earliest lessons I learned is that even though the United States is supposed to be 'one nation indivisible,' it's really a bunch of little nations, all with their own distinct language and interpretation of history. A sow bug in California is a 'roly-poly' in Arkansas. What half the country calls a civil war, the other half remembers as a fight between two sovereign powers. I never knew what to expect. For a girl already self-conscious about being different, desperately wanting to blend in, it was often . . . disconcerting."

She paused, remembering, and Brandt watched troubled images flicker in her eyes. After a moment her face cleared, and her mouth curved poignantly. "But at the same time I was living like a Gypsy, I also learned that the circumference of a circle equals *pi* times the diameter, whether you're in Mobile or Minneapolis, and two plus two always equals four, no matter what accent the teacher has. I found great comfort in that fact."

"Was your life really so unsettled?" Brandt asked, hoping she was exaggerating.

"Until my parents died it was," she stated simply. "After that everything changed. Mike was only eighteen, and there was no way the authorities were going to allow him to take me on the road the way our parents had done. So rather than let me be placed in a foster home while he pursued his musical career alone, he postponed his own plans and got a job in a vegetable cannery.

"As for me, I kept house, baby-sat my trig teacher's twins on weekends, and for the first time in my life attended the same school for a full year. Since we'd never had anything much even when our parents were alive, I didn't mind that money was tight. In fact—and I know this sounds awful—once I'd gotten over the first shock of losing Mom and Dad, I realized I'd never been more content."

"But your brother wasn't?" Brandt queried acutely.

She sighed. "I had no idea how much he missed his music. He never complained. While I finished high school with honors and won my scholarship to Sac State, Mike supported the two of us with jobs he hated. He packed tomatoes and drove a delivery truck at night. In what little free time he had, he kept up his music by forming a combo and playing the cornet. That was the beginning of the New Helvetia Jazz Society. I was having the time of my life, studying, dating, while he—" Meredith shrugged. "Anyway, things came to a head during my junior year, and I finally realized how unhappy he was. I knew it was time for me to take over supporting us, so that he could pursue his own dreams."

"And that's when you dropped out of college?"

"I had to. I owed him."

Brandt listened with mixed emotions. Despite Meredith's understandable gratitude for the way her brother had raised her, he wasn't certain he agreed with her conclusion that it was up to her to finance the man's musical career. The idea of her supporting an able-bodied male who must be nearly thirty made him uneasy.

Still, he admitted, he was impressed by the motives that drove her. That kind of devotion was rare. He wouldn't mind having some of it directed at himself. "You're a special woman, Meredith," he saluted her gravely. "You're loving and loyal. I admire that very much."

"Why, thank you," Meredith said, touched. "What a lovely thing to—"

Brandt lifted his arm from behind her neck and gently removed her glasses. "Let me show you how much." Folding the earpieces carefully, he set the glasses on the coffee table.

Meredith blinked owlishly, growing tense as spectral blurred images filled her universe. Suddenly apprehensive, she blurted, "Brandt, starting Monday we're going to be working together. Is this a good idea?"

"Probably not," he conceded lightly. He lowered his head until his face was in focus again. His arms wrapped around her with reassuring strength. "In fact," he breathed, "as far as office discipline is concerned, it's probably a very bad idea."

"Then why—"

"Because right now I think work is the farthest thing from either of our minds." Catching her chin in his fingertips, he guided her mouth to his.

His kiss was soft, she discovered. When his lips grazed hers, their touch was gentle, almost delicate, a whisper of warmth on her moist, sensitive skin. His mustache tickled, inviting her to open to his exploration. Meredith smiled. But when her lips parted, instead of pressing his advantage Brandt's mouth slid sideways, feathering along the line of her cheekbone, brushing aside her thick hair to nuzzle the tender skin behind her ear. She shivered at the erotic contact.

Every part of her was new, she thought dizzily, clinging to him with astonished fervor as the tremors of sensation he aroused arrowed along her nerves into her chest, her breasts. She had thought she was a woman of experience, but she had never been touched like this before. No man had ever melted her with his heat as Brandt was doing. He made her feel new-minted, bright. When he shifted her weight, pulling her onto his lap so that she lay across his thighs, she wound her arms around his neck and tried to draw him into the flames with her.

"Sweet, so sweet," Brandt sighed against her lips, his fingers fumbling with the buttons on her blouse. Just as the first one parted from its buttonhole, a key rattled in the lock on the front door of the apartment. Without warning the door flew open and Mike barged in.

4

"OH, HELL!" Brandt growled against Meredith's ear. His hands fell to her waist.

"Merry, you're never going to believe it!" Mike called, locking the door behind him. "You were right all along. That crazy kid Cheryl was only eighteen—*eighteen*! Of all the stupid, childish stunts! The last thing I need is the outraged father of some teenager—" After securing the door, he turned and for the first time looked into the living room.

"Oops!" Flabbergasted, Mike gaped at the couple entwined on the sofa.

Meredith giggled and waved a limp hand. Even with her blurred vision she could see her brother flush scarlet and quickly avert his eyes. "Hi, Mike," she greeted weakly.

"Sorry, sorry!" he muttered, scurrying into the hallway. The abashed apology was covered by the slam of the bathroom door.

Heaving a disgruntled sigh, Meredith said, "I'm sorry, Brandt, but he told me he'd probably be out all night."

"Apparently his plans changed."

"Apparently." She slid off his lap and reached for her glasses. When she could see again, she glanced down to check the fastenings on her shirt.

With efficient movements Brandt's fingers relooped the one loose button. "You're decent," he assured her.

"More's the pity," Meredith added with a grin.

After a second Brandt observed mildly, "Most roommates arrange some kind of signal for when they want privacy. In my college dorm, as I recall, it was usually a necktie wrapped around the doorknob. I'm a little surprised you and your brother haven't worked out something similar."

Tossing her head so that her hair fell away from her face, Meredith drew her knees up under her chin and wrapped her arms around her legs. She forced a smile. "Actually," she noted, "I don't think the need's ever arisen before." When Brandt's brows shot up skeptically, Meredith appended, "No, I don't mean that the way you're probably thinking. Mike and I each lead perfectly normal lives. But we're both rather private people, and through tact or maybe just habit, the apartment has become sort of sacrosanct. We never bring our . . . friends home with us."

"Until tonight," Brandt corrected.

Regarding him steadily, Meredith nodded. "That's right. Until tonight."

"Is there some significance to my being the exception that I ought to be aware of?" he probed.

Her eyes drilled into his. "I honestly have no idea." Their gazes held, and Meredith realized that beneath her outward composure she was still as aroused as she had been before her brother blundered in. Quickly she looked away. She wondered how Brandt felt.

Exhaling gustily, she said, "Oh, well, since I've always questioned the wisdom of office romances, under the circumstances it's probably just as well things didn't go any further."

"If you say so." Brandt's voice was a dark grumble, but when Meredith glanced at him, his eyes were gleaming. He shook with silent laughter at the ribald absurdity of the situation. "The girl your brother picked up turned out to be a teenager?"

Meredith felt a giggle well in her own throat. "Poor Mike. I tried to tell him she was lying about her age, but he didn't believe me. He must have really had a shock when he found out the truth."

"But I'll bet it wasn't half as bad as the one he got when he walked in on us." Brandt reached across the back of the sofa and patted her shoulder consolingly. "Next time," he suggested, "maybe you'd better let me pick the place!"

She nodded happily. Next time sounded like a promise.

"I guess you might as well meet the other half of the family," she said. Lifting her head she sang, "Hey, Mike, you can quit hiding in the bathroom!"

When Mike ambled slowly back into the living room, his Byronic features composed but reserved, Brandt rose to his feet. Meredith stood, too, and she felt his arm slide familiarly around her waist. Together they met Mike's curious gaze. After a moment she intoned, "Mike, I'd like you to meet Brandt Dahlberg. Brandt, this is my brother, Michael Forrester, head of the family—or so he thinks—and founder of the New Helvetia Jazz Society."

The two men regarded each other gravely. Extending his free hand, Brandt said, "I'm delighted to meet you, Mike. I've had the pleasure of hearing your band several times."

"Always glad to meet a fan," Mike murmured. As he shook Brandt's hand, his hazel eyes narrowed in recognition. "Aren't you the guy who was sitting at the back of Sonora Sue's tonight, the one Merry was staring at?" He turned to his sister. "And you claimed you couldn't see anything because you were wearing your contact lenses!"

Meredith felt her cheeks prickle. "I couldn't. I didn't realize it was Brandt until after we finished the set."

Mike looked surprised. "Then you two already knew each other?"

"Starting Monday, Meredith will be working for me," Brandt volunteered.

"Working for you?"

"Yes. At Warcom Electronics. She's going to be my assistant."

"Warcom?" Mike repeated, puzzled. "Oh, the desk job. I didn't realize that was settled. She must have forgotten to tell me."

Meredith felt Brandt stiffen. She glared at her brother. "Getting this wonderful job was the reason I was so excited this afternoon," she reminded him with studied emphasis. "If you'd cared enough to ask, you would have known."

At last her piercing stare penetrated Mike's tactlessness. "Oh—oh, of course!" he declared, grinning ruefully. "I'm sorry, I didn't mean to be rude. But you have to understand, Brandt, that in the final analysis, music is the only thing that really matters to us Forresters."

"Meredith did tell me the two of you have been performing professionally since childhood."

"Oh, yeah, we come by it naturally," Mike agreed, gazing fondly at his sister. "Mom and Dad died before they got their break, but it's not going to be that way for Merry and me. Someday some promoter or record company executive is going to spot us, and then it'll be goodbye Sacramento, hello big time."

"You don't say." As Mike gushed, Brandt's replies became curt, clipped.

Mike continued blithely. "Who knows? Maybe our break will come when we appear at the jazz festival this year. It's happened before. That young actress Molly Ringwald used to sing at the Jubilee."

"Really?"

"Oh, sure. Her father's band—"

With dismay Meredith felt Brandt's arm fall away from her waist. When she looked at him, at the tall, forbidding figure with golden hair still tousled from her fingertips, she had trouble believing he was the same man who had kissed and caressed her only moments before.

He glanced down at her. "You *are* going to be able to start work Monday?"

"Yes, of course," she answered, confused. "Now that the tax deadline is past, there's not so much call for part-time bookkeepers. Anyway, the agency is used to people dropping off their lists."

"Just like that?" *So much for dedication to her work*, he thought drearily. When he departed a few minutes later, his exit was punctiliously formal. He did not kiss Meredith goodbye.

The instant the door closed behind him, she whirled on her brother. Her eyes were full of fury and frustration as she railed, "Damn you, Michael David Forrester, you have the sensitivity of a rhinoceros! What do you mean, chasing him off that way?"

Mike looked affronted. "Now wait a minute, Merry. How was I supposed to know you were bringing some guy home with you? The least you could have done was warn me."

"Oh, really? And exactly how did you expect me to do that, after the way you left me stranded? I was stuck in the middle of Old Sacramento, dressed like a hooker and fending off winos, while you and some adolescent groupie—"

Holding up his palm like a traffic policeman—or a stern big brother, she thought grudgingly—Mike silenced her. "Wait a minute, Merry, what's this about winos?"

In a couple of brief sentences Meredith related the incident on the Embarcadero. When she finished, Mike said gravely, "I'm sorry, hon. It's my fault. Before I left with Don and the girls, I should have made sure you got home safely. I promise it won't happen again." He paused. Glancing uncertainly toward the sofa with its tumbled cushions, he ventured, "Then that little scene I interrupted was just your way of showing your gratitude for the way your new boss came to your rescue?"

"Of course not!" Meredith wasn't sure whether she ought to feel insulted or just impatient. Knowing her brother, she settled on the latter. "Mike," she said with a reproving sigh, "apart from the fact that I didn't need to be rescued, you ought to realize I'd never use my body to pay back a favor of any kind."

Mike looked relieved. "Well, I didn't think you would, but I had to be sure. Sometimes I have the feeling I just don't understand you anymore."

Meredith shrugged. "Forget it. Let's just change the subject, okay? Tell me what happened when you went to the ad agency in San Francisco this morning. Did they like the demo tape?"

A few weeks before, on the recommendation of Jack Barnes, Mike had composed a sprightly radio jingle for a local automobile dealer, which he had then recorded with his band. The dealer had been so delighted with the commercial that he suggested Mike mail a tape of it to the advertising agency that handled the regional account for his particular motor company, in the hope that the jingle might air all over northern California.

"The people at the agency liked the tape so much they offered me a job on the strength of it," Mike said glumly.

Meredith squealed with delight. "Oh, Mike, that's wonderful!" Since her brother quit his job at the cannery, his only income had been his cut of whatever the band earned playing cocktail lounges, pizza parlors or the occasional wedding. Although he was scrupulous about sharing what little money he did make, and although Meredith sincerely did not mind being the breadwinner in the family, she knew it would be a relief to have him bringing in a regular salary once more. "I'm so happy for you."

"I turned it down."

"You did what?"

"The money they talked about was tempting, but I turned them down. I had to."

Meredith sank weakly onto the sofa. "I don't understand. I thought the only thing you ever wanted out of life was a job in the music industry."

"In the music industry," Mike agreed. "But this would be advertising. They're looking for an in-house composer, someone who can crank out melodies in twenty-second chunks to back up their commercials for tacos or toilet paper. The pay's good, but the work would be anonymous and impersonal—almost as bad as being a studio musician."

"Paul Williams and Barry Manilow both started out scoring commercials. You could hardly call either of them anonymous." Meredith reminded her brother.

"No, but they're both solo acts." Mike shook his head emphatically. His eyes were intent, and a lock of dark hair fell in a comma across his pale forehead. Watching him, it occurred to Meredith that Mike's brooding good looks were at odds with the style of music he played; he should have been a balladeer.

Seriously he said, "Look, hon, I've always accepted the fact that I'd have to leave the band someday. After all, except for Don, the other guys all have families here in Sacramento. To them jazz is just a hobby. They're certainly not going to disrupt their lives because I get an offer in the

Bay area. But what about us? You and I are the only family we have. We've always depended on each other. If I take a full-time job in San Francisco, are you ready to go with me? What happens to us?"

"You'll work for your ad agency in San Francisco, and I'll work for Warcom here. It's no big deal." The distress that played across her brother's features as she spoke reminded Meredith too late how callous and uncaring she must sound to him. Smiling reassuringly she declared, "Mike, you and I will always be family. We'll always be close, even if we live halfway around the world from each other! It's true we've depended on each other since we were children, but we're adults now, independent adults. And in the final analysis, the only reason we've stayed together as long as we have is because there's never been any overriding reason not to. If, for example, one of us had fallen in love and decided to get married, we would have gone our separate ways years ago."

"But what about our plans? What about Mom and Dad's dream of making the Forrester name famous throughout the musical world?"

At the mention of the dark man with the banjo, the woman whose fall of crimson hair had smouldered like the sultry songs she played on her clarinet, Meredith blinked. That giddy, loving couple were now only a poignant memory she hadn't called to mind in a long time, and she was surprised when she felt unshed tears sting her eyes. Thickly she said, "Mike, Mom and Dad are dead."

Her brother's tone matched her own. "I know, Merry, I know. They died too damn young, with all their ambitions unfulfilled. That's why you and I owe it to them not to let their dream die, too."

SOMETIME OVER THE WEEKEND a reserved parking space had magically appeared in the Warcom lot, with the name M. Forrester painted on the concrete bumper. As Meredith slid her Toyota into the slot Monday morning, she observed that beside it was an empty space designated B. Dahlberg, the same space she'd noticed vacant on Friday, when she arrived for her interview. She wondered if Brandt ever drove his sleek Volvo to work.

There was no sign of him or his ten-speed, although while she was locking her car several helmeted cyclists glided down from the bike trail. They greeted her amiably, dismounting and chaining their bikes to the steel racks embedded in the pavement near the side entrance to the plant. Meredith returned their casual greetings with a nod and followed them inside. The group divided by sexes and ducked into twin doors marked Lockers and Showers. Meredith could hear running water and convivial voices echoing hollowly off ceramic-tiled surfaces. Farther down the hall she noticed parents ushering small children through a door labeled Day Care. She smiled. Despite the utilitarian decor of the lower floors, Warcom obviously provided a lot of amenities for its staff. It was going to be a good company ' work for.

She reported to the executive suite where Lois Nelson greeted her, her smile warm and genuine. "I'm so glad you're going to be with us. It'll be nice to have some young blood around here." She handed over a security badge and a sheaf of official-looking documents that had been lying beside her word processor, explaining that they were the usual tax and insurance forms.

While Meredith signed each sheet of paper, Lois also asked if she would like to be assigned a locker in the shower room. Declining with thanks, Meredith clipped the badge to the jacket of her lilac-colored suit.

Lois chirped, "That's a pretty outfit. I like the color. It's very striking with your beautiful hair. The reason I asked about the locker is that many employees bike or jog to work and change on the grounds. Hardly anyone but Walter or Mr. Dahlberg dress formally—for seeing clients, you understand. I can't tell you how glad we are you're taking the job! Ever since Mr. Dahlberg's assistant ran off to that swami in Oregon he's been more impossible than ever. It's gotten to the point where Annette Nakatani refuses to loan him any more of her clerical people. But I'm sure with you here, things will soon be back to normal."

"I'll do whatever I can," Meredith said neutrally. She wondered with a mixture of apprehension and anticipation whether relations between her and Brandt Dahlberg could ever be called normal. They'd progressed far beyond the usual employer-employee relationship the first day they met.

She was pushing the completed forms back across the desk when she heard the door to the inner office open. A heavy footfall sounded behind her and a booming voice declared, "Ah, the radiant Ms Forrester! I thought it was you." Meredith turned with pleasure to say hello. The word stopped in her throat. Burly and bearded, his gaze bright and twinkling, Walter Warren loomed over her like the friendly giant from a fairy tale, even taller and broader than she remembered. Once again he was in his shirt sleeves, his tie already loosened despite the fact the workday had only just begun.

What she could not comprehend was the incongruous vision of Walter's massive hand delicately grasping the end of a long scarlet ribbon, the other end of which was attached to a heart-shaped balloon, at least two feet wide. The shining silver object bobbed and bounced on the air currents just above Walter's bald head.

Meredith gaped, then glanced furtively at Lois, but she was beaming benignly, watching the scene. Hesitantly Meredith faced her new boss again. The instant her eyes met his, he bowed with surprising grace and presented the ribbon to her. "For you, my dear," he announced, giving a devilish grin. "Welcome to Warcom."

"Thank you," Meredith murmured automatically as she accepted the balloon. She felt her own spirits lift when the puffy heart swayed and tugged on the ribbon.

Walter perceived her confusion. "It's just my oddball way of telling you I hope you'll be happy working for my company," he explained. "Flowers are so banal."

"Well, thank you," Meredith said again, this time with more conviction. "I'm sure—" The telephone rang, cutting her off in midsentence.

Lois picked up the receiver, her greeting crisp and businesslike. Listening for a moment, she responded, "Yes, Mr. Dahlberg, she's here, talking to Mr. Warren. Of course, sir, I'll send her at once." Lois glanced reproachfully at Walter when she hung up. "Your second in command is getting all hot under the collar."

"And it's all my fault for keeping her here." Walter's tone was noticeably unrepentant. "Meredith, I guess you'd better hustle. Brandt's office is the first one on the left, halfway down the hall. Don't lose your balloon."

How could anyone lose the balloon, Meredith wondered as she headed along the corridor, the heart floating after her like an airborne valentine. Walter's gesture had been whimsical and disarming, but at a moment when Meredith had intended to be her most businesslike and professional, she felt like a cartoon symbol of romance.

But, then, perhaps she didn't look as foolish as she felt. Before she reached the door to Brandt's office she passed a woman going in the opposite direction, a stack of ma-

nila folders in her arms. Dressed in a khaki safari suit and
canvas espadrilles, the woman appeared to be in her late
thirties. She glanced at the balloon, grinned and said easily, "Hi! You must be new here. I can see Walter's wel-
comed you to the fold." While her straight black hair and
almond eyes proclaimed her Oriental ancestry, her accent
and her firm, athletic stride were pure Californian. Shifting the folders to the crook of one arm, she stuck out her
hand and announced, "I'm Annette Nakatani, head of
clerical."

"Hi. Meredith Forrester. I'm the new personal assistant
to Brandt Dahlberg."

Annette's finely arched brows rose and she surveyed
Meredith again. "So you're the champion who's been sent
to save my girls from the dreaded Dahlberg. I hope you're
good on a bicycle."

Meredith looked at her in blank dismay. "Oh, no, you
mean—"

"Actually, I just meant Brandt Dahlberg's a hard man
to keep up with. Very quick and fair but demanding. On
the other hand, it might be useful to keep a bicycle nearby
in case someday you want to make a hasty escape." Noting Meredith's startled expression, Annette clucked reassuringly. "Oh, don't mind me. Brandt's a nice guy, and I'm
sure you're going to enjoy working with him." She glanced
at her watch. "I have to go now, but if you're planning to
eat lunch in the cafeteria, we'll probably run into each
other then. If you like, I'll save you a spot at my table."

"Thank you. That would be nice."

"Fine. See you."

Meredith watched with a smile as the other woman disappeared into her office. Annette's warmth only reinforced her conviction that her life was taking a turn for the
better. A good, challenging job in pleasant surroundings

with congenial co-workers: what more could she ask for?
Plus she would be working with the most attractive man
she'd ever known.

A second, smaller brass plate had appeared beneath
Brandt's on the door. Meredith grinned. She'd never had
her name on a door before. Stepping inside, she found
herself in a vacant outer office. Surprisingly spacious, the
room's decor was plush but impersonal; the beige walls
looked as though they were waiting for her to stamp her
personality upon them. She decided at once that she'd
bring in some plants and perhaps one or two of her framed
jazz festival posters. Then she noticed the connecting door
to Brandt's office; it was open. When she stepped toward
it, her feet felt as light as the balloon she carried.

His office was much larger than hers, bright and airy. A
leather sofa ran the length of the wall opposite the desk.
On the wall above the sofa was an assortment of sporting
prints depicting nineteenth-century European bicycle
races. Next to a door that was open to reveal a dressing
room and bath, was a glass cabinet full of cycling trophies. For the first time Meredith realized Brandt's interest in the sport went beyond a desire for exercise.

He did not appear to notice her at first. He was seated
behind a massive desk of burled walnut, its beautiful grain
dark with age. Leaning back in the matching swivel chair,
he absently combed his mustache with his fingers. He was
frowning at a computer terminal, which seemed utterly
out of place amid the antique furniture.

Meredith was surprised at his choice of decor; she would
have guessed he'd like the high-tech look. What surprised
her even more was the instant hunger she felt at the sight
of Brandt.

Over the weekend she had wondered if his allure would
diminish once she'd recovered from the shock of the der-

elict's assault and the combined effects of music, alcohol
and a sultry spring night. She knew, of course, that come
Monday morning he'd still be attractive to her. But she had
thought perhaps she would be able to observe his physical beauty with the same indifferent appreciation she felt
for handsome movie actors. Apparently not.

Through a picture window overlooking a panorama of
the American River, sunlight beamed in and danced in
Brandt's fair hair, limned the sharp, compelling lines of his
profile. Meredith caught her breath. Gazing at that lanky
athletic body, the golden tan emphasized by the crisp,
snowy shirt he wore, she wanted him.

Just as she lifted her fist to tap on the doorjamb, he
swung around abruptly. His gaze skimmed over her, taking in the prim lilac suit she wore and the sleek French twist
by which she'd subdued her unruly hair. Then he spotted
the silver balloon. His mouth tightened.

Straightening in his chair, he said flatly, "I'm glad Walter's made you feel welcome. One of the prerogatives of
being the boss is that you can take time for frivolities like
floating hearts, but I hope that in the future you'll remember you're working for me, not him. Now please go do
something with that toy so we can get started. We have a
lot of catching up to do."

By THE END of the first day, Brandt suspected Meredith
thought he was deliberately snubbing her. By the end of
the first week, he was certain of it.

He could see her confusion and hurt growing daily. He
knew that even under the best of circumstances he was not
an easy man to work for—demanding, impatient with in-
competence—but that was only because he cared about
Warcom. He wanted the company his father and Walter
had built to continue to thrive. He never asked anything

of the rest of the staff that he was unwilling to do himself.
Everyone knew that no matter how tyrannical he might
appear in the office, it was nothing personal. . . .

Everyone knew except Meredith. She'd seen him with
other personnel—Lois and the stenographers and key data
entry people in Annette's department—chuckling over
Walter's latest gag or discussing an upcoming bicycle race.
She'd obviously compared his warmth in the staff lounge
with his reserve behind his desk, and she'd taken the contrast personally. She thought he did not want her there.

The hell of it was, Brandt admitted glumly, in a way she
was right. Life would have been so much simpler if only
Walter had not convinced Brandt to hire her. If only they'd
met, say, at Sonora Sue's. Two strangers drawn together
by mutual attraction and a fondness for classic jazz would
have no professional conflicts to hinder their relationship. But as it was, he didn't know how he was supposed
to concentrate on his job when the most appealing woman
he'd met in years kept flitting in and out of his office, her
unique perfume wafting in her wake.

The problem didn't end there, however, because as attracted to Meredith as he was on a personal level, Brandt
was still skeptical of her professional qualifications and her
dedication to her job. After that discussion with her
brother Friday night, Brandt couldn't flatter himself that
she'd favor working at Warcom over a shot at show business. No matter how strongly she protested, Meredith was
too talented and too vibrant to bury herself for long among
semiconductors and computer printouts.

Cynthia had sworn that being Brandt's wife was all the
career she'd ever want. Within a year she'd left him to
dance in a revue in Reno and, incidentally, file for divorce. One of these days Meredith was undoubtedly going
to make a similar decision. And in the meantime, Brandt

didn't know which would be worse: wanting her and not touching her, or touching her and knowing it couldn't last.

"WILL THERE BE anything else, sir?" Meredith asked stiffly of the man hovering at her shoulder. The afternoon was unseasonably hot, and Brandt had discarded his coat and tie and unbuttoned his collar. The wings of starched cotton folded back, uncovering his strong, corded throat. Meredith tried not to recall how hard yet oddly smooth his tanned skin had felt beneath her fingertips.

"It's almost five," he noted, "but I was wondering if you'd finished evaluating those readouts I asked you to look at?"

"Yes, sir." Instantly she was all business. Flipping through a fanfolded computer listing, she ran the tip of her pencil down the columns of figures as she spoke. "The data is clear enough. If all you want to know is whether this component can handle the increased power requirements of your new disk drive, as presently designed, then the answer's yes. But while I was studying the various test results, something occurred to me. If you follow this curve, you'll see—" In the margin of the page she sketched a rough graph to illustrate her observations.

Brandt leaned over the back of her chair, his brow furrowed as he listened intently. He did not touch her, but she could feel his warmth radiating across the charged gap between them. "So you're suggesting we ought to redesign the component now because if we don't, we'll have problems later when we try to upgrade?"

"I'm not suggesting anything," Meredith replied evenly, trying to ignore his nearness as she craned her neck to look up into his face. "All I do is translate the figures you give me. Value judgments are your department."

Brandt was silent for several moments while he stared at the green-barred paper. At last he nodded. "I think you're on to something. I'd better show these to Walter on Monday."

When he reached over her shoulder to pick up the printouts, his fingers brushed the curve of her breast. Meredith froze. Carefully Brandt pulled away, saying, "You've done a good job, Meredith. Thank you."

"You're welcome." Her voice trembled, not from his nearness but from surprise. His compliment seemed to be almost the first civil words he'd spoken to her in the office since she'd come to work for him.

She gazed up at him, waiting for him to gather his papers and leave. Still he hesitated. She saw him glance at the framed posters ornamenting her walls on either side of a lush Boston fern in a macramé hanger. One of them depicted Old Sacramento in a halo of flames, with the legend A Hot Time in the Old Town Tonight.

Although Annette and Lois had both commented enthusiastically on the way Meredith had begun to decorate her office, Brandt had studiously ignored her efforts until now. His eyes dropped to the framed photograph at the corner of her desk. An eight-by-ten glossy, it was obviously some kind of publicity shot: a couple in their early thirties, an adolescent boy and a wide-eyed little girl with freckles and wing-tipped glasses. All wore matching plaid vests, and everyone except the little girl carried a musical instrument. "Your family?" Brandt asked unnecessarily.

Meredith nodded. "It's not my favorite picture, but it's the only one I could find with all four of us together. And I wanted . . ." Her voice trailed off; she was afraid she sounded maudlin.

"And you wanted some part of your family, some token of home with you," Brandt softly finished for her. "I understand exactly how you feel. That oversize desk of mine used to belong to my grandfather. I can remember doing homework at it when I was so small I had to sit on a dictionary.

"When I took over my father's place here at Warcom, the movers had to hoist the desk up the side of the building and bring it in through the picture window. I told Walter I didn't care if they had to knock down a wall. That desk was important to me, and if I was going to spend half my waking life in that office, then I intended to spend it behind Grandpa's desk."

Smiling wistfully, Meredith tried to imagine Brandt as a little boy. "It must be nice to have heirlooms," she murmured.

"You have other things that are just as important," Brandt said. "Memories, for example. My father and I were very happy together, but I'd give anything to be able to remember what my mother was like."

Before Meredith could reply, Brandt shook his head and conspicuously consulted his wristwatch. "Here I am rambling on, and it's well past quitting time. Shouldn't you be heading home to get ready for a performance or something?"

Startled by his abrupt change of mood, Meredith shook her head. "No."

"You're not singing tonight?"

"No," she repeated with a shrug. "The band's working at a pizza parlor, but they don't need a vocalist."

"And you don't mind?" he persisted.

She wondered what he was leading up to, and why he seemed so uncharacteristically diffident. "Mind?" she countered with a mirthless laugh. "Heavens, no. I hate gigs like that! In a way those places are worse than the bars. The audience keeps shifting, and there's invariably at least one squalling baby or a toddler whose parents think it's cute when he tries to climb onto the bandstand. And if a bunch of rowdy teenagers don't start bugging you just as you're building up to a wow finish on your song, then a voice comes over the loudspeaker and announces, 'Number 42, your anchovy pizza is ready.'"

Meredith smiled as if she was joking, but there was a cynical edge to her voice. She finished drearily, "No, I don't resent the fact that I won't be singing with my brother's band tonight. When I was a child, I was exposed to enough pizza parlors to put me off Italian food for life. Anyway, I'm tired. It's been a rough week."

Brandt nodded. "Yes, it has, hasn't it? In more ways than one. But perhaps things will be better from now on."

5

"SO WHEN DID YOU decide you don't want to be in the parade?" Mike demanded. "This is the first I've heard of it."

Meredith glanced at the other band members, who were studiously ignoring the conversation between brother and sister. One of them was replacing a broken banjo string, while the trombone player fiddled with the spit valve on his horn. Don and the pianist, whose garage was doubling as their rehearsal hall, had disappeared into the house, ostensibly to fetch something cool to drink.

The heavy atmosphere inside the stuffy garage had little to do with the heat. Meredith brushed aside the tendrils of hair that had escaped from her slightly lopsided topknot; the muscles at the back of her neck were beginning to throb. Pressing her fingertips into her nape, she tried to massage away the tension. She wished Mike would quit harping at her.

"So let us in on your reasons for not wanting to march with the rest of us in the parade that opens the Jubilee," he badgered. "The media coverage will be fantastic. TV and newspaper people are coming from all over the state."

Meredith shrugged. "What good would media coverage do me? You and the guys may be able to play while you walk, but I certainly can't sing."

"But that's not the point, Merry! Whether or not you sing, you're a member of the band. You belong with us. After all these years of being on the outside looking in, wanting to be part of the jazz festival, I can't understand why you'd want to pass up even one event. Just think of all the greats who've marched there before us—everyone from Eubie Blake to Bob Crosby. And now we, the New Helvetia Jazz Society, have the privilege of strutting down that very same street—"

"I do not strut," Meredith stated.

Her brother tossed back, "You don't do much of anything these days, do you? Certainly not where the band's concerned. Ever since you got that new job, it's all you can think about."

Meredith bridled. "That's not true. It's only because of my new job that you and I are able to foot our share of the rental for the recording studio we've booked. I'm certainly doing my part to make sure you'll have tapes ready to hand out to all those agents and promoters you hope to meet during the festival!"

"All right, all right!" Mike held up his hands in a gesture of surrender. "I'm sorry, Merry, I was out of line. I know where money's involved, you've been more than generous. I appreciate it, I really do, and I promise I'll pay you back just as soon as possible. But I still say you were a lot more enthusiastic about our music when you were just a part-time bookkeeper. Have you forgotten how much the festival might mean to us? You know as well as I do that this could be our big break. Sometimes I wonder if you even give a damn anymore. Hell, you seem to care less about the Jubilee than you do about this birthday party your office is throwing for the head honcho."

"Walter Warren is a friend," Meredith said. "And if you'd—"

"Hey, you two, give it a rest, will you?" Don cut in as he and the pianist reappeared at the door, lugging between them a foam cooler full of crushed ice and chilling cans.

The clarinet player regarded the siblings impatiently. "Cripes, I haven't heard so much bickering and backbiting since my twin sisters both fell for the shortstop on the high school baseball team. Here, shut up and have a beer."

Accepting the frost-beaded can, Meredith popped the ring and leaned back against the garage wall. As the cold liquid trickled refreshingly down her throat, she grimaced, not from the bitter taste of the malty brew but from the realization that Don was right. She and Mike were squabbling like a couple of teenagers. They'd been quarreling and snapping at each other for days. She couldn't imagine why. Normally they were fondly tolerant of each other's foibles. But now . . .

Of course Meredith was perfectly aware why her own temper was so short. As much as she enjoyed her work at Warcom, sometimes the frustration of being around Brandt was almost unbearable. She itched to touch him, but her dignity demanded she pretend indifference. By the end of the day she usually came home ready to bite someone. But Mike was not like her; his attitude toward everything except music was casual to the point of being phlegmatic. She couldn't imagine what could bug him enough to make him as testy as she was.

As if in answer to her unspoken question, Don sidled up to Meredith and muttered under his breath, "Ease up on Mike, will you, Merry? He's got woman problems."

Astonished, she glanced sidelong at the clarinet player, but he shook his head warningly and did not expand on his statement. Meredith gazed through her lashes at her brother. Woman problems? She'd had no idea; Mike had given no sign, no hint. She hadn't even realized he was seeing anyone except that Cheryl person, and he'd dropped her the instant he learned her real age. Meredith

wondered why he was keeping the new relationship a secret.

She had had her fill of secrets lately. Warcom was buzzing with them. Lois Nelson was organizing a company
birthday party for Walter, who would turn sixty on the last
day of April, and her efforts to keep the festivities a surprise were becoming a bit tiresome, if not ludicrous.
Sometimes the arrangements reminded Meredith of a bad
spy novel. Surreptitious memos, passed from department to department, were wadded and dropped in waste-
baskets if Walter walked into a room; interoffice phone
calls terminated abruptly whenever he opened a door. As
much as Meredith liked Walter's secretary, she honestly
did not see how the woman expected to invite three
hundred employees to a gala celebration in the Warcom
cafeteria without her boss getting at least an inkling that
something was afoot. She said as much one morning while
she and Brandt shared a coffee break in his office.

Leaning back in his swivel chair, he stared out the picture window at the vista spread before him, the gleaming
copper-topped dome of the California state capitol rising
above the trees in the distance beyond the river. Mildly he
observed, "Of course Walter already knows what's going
on. Probably even knows the exact time and place of the
party, but he'd never spoil Lois's plans by letting on. He
wouldn't want to hurt her feelings."

"I guess he realizes how much the surprise means to her,"
Meredith concluded. While she sipped her coffee she relaxed on the wide leather sofa opposite the desk and gazed
in Brandt's direction. She loved to look at him; there was
sensual gratification to be derived from just that.

After the first tense week, their relationship had relaxed, become more amicable. Neither of them mentioned the convulsive passion that had gripped them in the

beginning. Now in the office they worked together harmoniously, with mutual respect for each other's skills. What hurt Meredith was that they did not see each other outside the office.

She sighed. "Well, I'm glad Walter appreciates the effort Lois is making for him. She's a very devoted secretary."

Brandt's mouth twisted into a wry smile. "She's in love with him," he said simply. When Meredith's eyes widened, he added deliberately, "What's more, Walter's in love with Lois."

"If that's the case, then I don't understand why they haven't done something about it. They're two warm, caring people—"

"Walter is married."

Carefully Meredith balanced her coffee cup on the arm of the sofa. "Perhaps you'd better explain."

Brandt shrugged. "There's not a whole lot to explain. His wife is a permanent resident at a retreat near Lake Tahoe, a posh sanitarium, really. She's been there for years. Chronic schizophrenia. Physically she's well and with medication she's able to live a fairly normal life inside the retreat. She gets the best care money can buy, but she's never going to be able to function in the outside world again."

"How tragic," Meredith breathed, horrified.

"Yes, it is tragic. For everyone," Brandt agreed. "Once I went to Tahoe with Walter to visit her. She's a lovely woman, seems quite lucid at first, but if you exchange more than two sentences with her, you realize she's immersed in her own little dreamworld. I'm not sure she really knew we were there. At the same time, it was obvious that Walter felt only the pity anyone would feel for someone in that condition—pity and guilt."

"Guilt?"

Brandt nodded grimly. "Walter blames himself for his wife's condition. Her illness came on gradually, and he says if he hadn't been so busy building up Warcom he might have realized what was happening in time to help her.... I don't know how justified his remorse is. I do know that he and Lois could make each other very happy. But Walter feels too much obligation toward his wife ever to divorce her, and he loves Lois too much ever to offer her less than marriage."

Meredith thought sadly of the brilliant engineer with the childish delight in games and pranks, loving one woman, tied to another he once loved who could no longer provide either comfort or companionship. Maybe Walter Warren was a classic example of the clown who laughed to hide a broken heart. She wondered as she watched the determined glee with which he opened his presents at the party.

When Lois had lured him into the darkened cafeteria, supposedly to help her search for a missing notebook, three hundred voices had bellowed "Surprise!" Walter's reaction had been big and loud, expansive as the man himself.

Perhaps too much so, Meredith decided. In a flurry of balloons and streamers he proclaimed his absolute astonishment that his employees had been able to organize such an event without his having the slightest suspicion. They all came forward then to wish him well and to press gifts upon him. He clapped men on their shoulders and kissed the women exuberantly...most of the women. To Lois he gravely and hesitantly extended his hand, drawing back the instant their fingers met, almost as if he was afraid to touch her.

Seating herself on the edge of one of the tables, Meredith watched the festivities with pleasure. A short time later she realized with a start that Brandt was no longer there. Wondering where on earth he could have gone, she scanned the assembly for a sight of his gleaming head. She noticed that Lois and Annette had disappeared, too.

Suddenly, the double doors at the end of the cafeteria flew open. Brandt and two janitors entered, dragging a cumbersome wheeled pallet loaded with something huge, swathed in white sheets. The mystery object was at least four feet wide and seven feet high, girdled by an enormous scarlet ribbon. Handing a pair of scissors to his partner, Brandt announced, "It's all yours, boss. The ultimate gadget. I thought of you the moment I spotted it in San Francisco. Hope you like it."

When the ribbons were snipped the sheets fell away, and a chorus of delighted oohs rose from the crowd. Meredith gasped. Brandt's gift to his friend was an antique nickelodeon—a coin-operated mechanical orchestra with cymbals, drums, bells and a player piano. Meredith was sure it had once graced a turn-of-the-century penny arcade.

For once Walter's grin was missing; he blinked, overwhelmed. "Brandt, it's beautiful. I—I don't know how to—" He glanced around. "Where's Lois?" he asked tremulously. "I want her to see—"

As if on his signal, the two missing women returned. They were pushing a cart bearing a vast cake ablaze with candles. Walter stared at Lois with misty amazement. "All you wonderful people," he murmured. "There just aren't any words—"

"So don't worry about the words," Brandt said. Even across the width of the room his love for his friend was obvious as he solemnly presented Walter a shiny coin.

"Just try out the nickelodeon. The first roll's already in place."

The older man's hands shook visibly as he dropped the coin in the slot. Inside the huge music box motors began to turn, unwinding a long reel of perforated parchment paper. Bellows pumped, bells clanged, a brassy fanfare sounded, and all at once the cafeteria echoed with the melody of "Happy Birthday."

Everyone joined in the song, their off-key harmonizing full of warmth and affection. Meredith sang with them, and it was only when she noticed several curious glances in her direction that she realized her trained voice carried clearly over the others in the crowd. Uncomfortable, she stopped singing.

Her silence came too late. As soon as he finished blowing out the candles with one gale of breath, Walter lifted his head and boomed, "Hey, I didn't know we had talent in our midst!"

Meredith shrank back, blushing, embarrassed that she had made herself conspicuous. So far nobody at Warcom was aware that she sometimes moonlighted as a singer—except Brandt, of course. Remembering his skepticism about her dedication to work, she had decided it would be wiser to keep her job and her avocation completely separate.

But Walter was sharp. He called, "Ms Forrester, that was you belting out 'Happy Birthday' like a professional?"

"Meredith *is* a professional singer," Brandt supplied matter-of-factly. "She's been performing since she was a child."

"Oh, really?" Lois exclaimed. Her surprise was reflected in the faces that turned to stare at Meredith. "I wish I'd known that before! I could have used some help with the entertainment."

Shaking her head, Meredith wondered why Brandt had revealed her secret. "I hardly think—"

Walter had been rummaging through a cardboard box that came with the nickelodeon. He interrupted, "Maybe she still can help you, Lois. There must be a dozen music rolls here. We can try out this marvelous machine—"

A chorus of voices cried encouragement. "Let's hear you, Meredith." Beckoning hands urged her forward, but still she hung back.

Walter glanced from Brandt to Meredith and then to Brandt again. As he rubbed his bald head, his mouth curved up in a teasing grin. "I had hoped she would want to sing just to please an old man on his birthday. But if that's not a good enough reason, well, Brandt, she's your assistant, and surely you—"

"Meredith doesn't have to do anything she doesn't want to," Brandt declined calmly but firmly. Seeing the surprise in her hazel eyes when they collided with his, he supposed she must have expected him to browbeat her. "The decision is yours, Merry Forrest," he assured her, his expression rueful. With a sigh Meredith wiped her palms on her linen slacks and slid off her perch on the edge of the table.

Brandt listened with appreciation as she began singing, but after a few moments his enjoyment faded. The tunes on the music rolls—pre-World War One favorites—had not been arranged for a soprano; she sounded as if her throat was growing raspy with the low keys and unnatural rhythms. By the time she choked off the final note of "The Band Played On," Brandt was scowling. Before someone could call for an encore, he stepped forward and switched off the nickelodeon.

"Thank you," she croaked, though the audience groaned its disappointment.

Walter, who had been engrossed in showing his presents to Lois, glanced up. "Over so soon? But I was enjoying the music."

"Everyone's anxious to hear the birthday boy make his speech," Brandt improvised. At once, encouraging voices confirmed his statement. Walter rose to his feet, and Brandt caught Meredith's wrist, easing her away from the center of the crowd. He did not stop gently propelling her until they stood at a drinking fountain in the quiet, empty corridor outside the cafeteria.

"Walter may know everything about silicon chips, but he's completely ignorant about vocalists," Brandt explained. "He'd have let the others keep after you until you couldn't sing at all."

Gulping cold water, Meredith gasped, "In that case, thanks again. I guess this time I really did need rescuing. I wouldn't have minded entertaining at the party if I'd been prepared for it, but I wasn't warmed up or anything, and that can be such a strain." She swallowed, testing her dry throat. After another drink, she declared, "There, that's better, thank goodness. My brother would never forgive me if I hurt my voice this close to the Jubilee."

"Surely he'd be sorry if you hurt your voice any time?"

Meredith shrugged. "Well, of course he would, but right now things are a little touchy between the two of us. If I damage my throat, he's going to be convinced I've done it on purpose."

"It sounds to me as if you and your brother could use a little break from each other," Brandt observed.

"I expect we could. At least, I know I need a break. Between starting this new job and rehearsing with the band, there just don't seem to be enough hours in a day."

To Meredith's surprise, Brandt captured her chin with his hand, his fingertips pressing lightly against the line of her jaw as he turned her face from side to side. He frowned judiciously. "Tell me, do you ever get out in the sunshine? The weather's been glorious lately, but you look rather pale."

She tried not to react to his touch on her skin. "That pallor is natural to redheads," she dismissed shakily, "and I'd be pale even if I had been outside. I don't tan. All sunlight does for me is make my freckles stand out."

"Is that why you're always powdering your nose?" he asked. "I've often wondered why you'd want to cover that lovely skin. There's nothing wrong with freckles, you know."

Meredith's eyes widened at his compliment, then clouded. "You wouldn't say that if you'd been heckled about them all your life," she muttered, recalling the teasing and torment she'd endured as a child. "Red hair is bad enough, but in this country it's considered downright un-American not to have a clear complexion."

Brandt let his hand drop away. "I'm sorry. I had no idea."

"Of course you didn't. How could you possibly know? You're a gorgeous sun-bronzed, golden-haired hunk—the California ideal!"

There was a long pause, during which laughter filtered from the cafeteria into the silence that pervaded the corridor. At last Brandt's mouth slanted quizzically, and he drawled, "Meredith, my dear, am I supposed to be flattered or insulted by that crack?"

Suddenly she was aware of how she'd sounded. Clapping her hand to her mouth in dismay, she groaned, "Oh, Lord, I'm being a bitch, aren't I? I'm sorry. I didn't mean... Oh, hell. I must be under more of a strain than I realized."

Brandt's smile was droll. "Don't worry about it. It's a little tough to get angry at a woman for calling me a hunk."

"You are one, you know," Meredith said quietly. "I've thought so since the first moment I saw you."

His dimple deepened. "You mean when I was lying on the asphalt in the parking lot after you knocked me off my bike?" Meredith refused to react to his bantering, and after a moment Brandt continued lightly. "And speaking of bikes, I still think it would do you good to get outdoors for a change. There are a couple of spare cycles in the day-care center. Would you like to borrow one and go for a ride with me?"

Meredith blanched. "A ride? On a bicycle?"

"Of course. We could take the trail alongside the river. Have you ever been through the American River Parkway? The scenery's really beautiful there now, everything's lush and green. As warm as it's been, the elder trees and blackberry vines are already in bloom—"

"I couldn't," Meredith choked, floundering for an excuse. "My clothes. I don't keep an exercise outfit in a locker the way Annette and some of the other women—"

Brandt assessed her trim figure, noting the natural linen slacks and low-heeled shoes she wore. "There's no need to worry about clothes; I don't plan to change, and your outfit is probably more appropriate than my trousers and dress shirt. You'll do just fine for an easy ride, and I promise it will be an easy one. I'm not planning to challenge you to a race or anything. I thought we could just meander up the bike trail a couple of miles or so while you relax and get some fresh air."

Meredith pleaded. "But you don't understand."

"Understand what?"

"I don't know how to ride a bicycle."

For a moment Brandt did not seem to hear her. Then his brows arched sharply. "What did you say?"

Sheepishly she repeated, "I don't know how to ride a bicycle. I never learned."

"But everybody knows how to ride a bike! For heaven's sake, didn't your older brother ever teach you?"

"I'm not sure Mike knows how, either. When we were kids, our family was always on the move, living out of a station wagon half the time. There was no room or money for things like bikes. By the time we settled in Sacramento, Mike was driving a car."

Brandt shook his head in exasperation. "Good grief, Meredith, didn't you ever do anything the normal way when you were a child?" At her distressed expression, he quickly amended, "I mean, didn't you ever *play*? For that matter, do you ever do anything just for fun even now?"

"Of course I do," she protested indignantly, "all the time."

"When?" Brandt demanded. "I know for a fact that those long, hard hours you work with me in the office are no great joy. As far as I can tell, the rest of the time you spend rehearsing with your band, and you don't seem to get much enjoyment from your singing—"

"You're wrong. I like singing; it's performing that I'm tired of."

"Okay, I can accept that. But when was the last time you did something simply to amuse yourself?"

Meredith considered. "I went to a movie in March. . . ."

"That was last month. What have you done since for the sheer pleasure of doing it?"

For a moment she was silent; then her mouth curved into an impish grin. "Well, just a couple of weeks ago I kissed you."

"And was that a pleasure?" he asked hoarsely.

"You know it was."

Their gazes locked. He lifted his hand as if to touch her face, and Meredith thought he was going to kiss her again. Instead, she saw his eyes flick around them, surveying the empty corridor. Then he began to comb his mustache with his knuckles, a gesture that Meredith already recognized as indicating he was deep in thought. After a moment he dropped his hand and said briskly, "Well, my dear, it really is a good thing you happened to wear pants today, because you are about to get your first lesson in the art of cycling. Before sundown today you're going to be riding like an Olympic medalist."

"But, Brandt . . ."

"Don't argue with me." He tried to nudge her along the corridor. "I assure you learning to ride a bicycle is no big deal. Six-year-olds do it every day. And it's fun. Soon you'll be asking yourself why you ever wanted to drive a car."

Meredith hung back. "I'm not sure . . ."

"I am," Brandt countered with good-natured persistence, "and at Warcom I outrank you."

In matching tones Meredith retorted, "Riding bikes with the boss is not part of my job description!"

"I know, I know. The omission was an unfortunate oversight on my part." Brandt held out his hand again. "Please, Meredith?" he cajoled. "You really will enjoy it. I promise."

Meredith sighed her acquiescence. "Well. If you promise . . ." His fingers curled warmly and securely around hers, and she forgot to finish her sentence.

When they slipped into the day-care center, they found the children seated in a circle on the carpet, listening to a story. Several youngsters waved a greeting to Brandt before they returned their attention to the man who was reading. At a nearby table, the teacher who Meredith had first seen in the parking lot the day of her interview was preparing snacks. When she spotted the couple at the door, she tiptoed to them.

"Hi, Brandt," she whispered. "Party over already?"

In equally hushed tones he answered, "Oh, no. The last I saw, it was still going strong." He looked at the juice and crackers she was setting out. "If you like, I could have some of the birthday cake sent in for the kids."

The woman shook her head. "Thanks, but please, no. This bunch is already hyper enough without feeding them refined sugar!" She nodded toward a cot in the corner, and Meredith saw the reason they were speaking so quietly. A small boy napped, his tearstained face belligerent even in sleep. His short arms were clutched tightly around a grubby Garfield doll.

"It's been a traumatic afternoon. One of the girls tried to take his doll away, and they almost came to blows," the teacher explained. "But I think he'll be all right by the time his mother picks him up. Meanwhile, what may I do for you, Brandt?"

When Brandt walked away with the teacher, Meredith stayed beside the cot, gazing tenderly at the sleeping child. She watched him nuzzle into the toy cat's orange-and-black-striped plush coat and tried to recall whether she'd ever owned a stuffed animal. There had been a tinny one-octave xylophone; she could remember her father teaching her the scale. But as for dolls . . .

"The bike is all arranged," Brandt said softly when he returned. "All we have to do is go around to the storage shed in the playground." He glanced down at the little boy and smiled. "Typical male—very possessive of his toys," he said with a chuckle. "Although I suppose little girls can be that way, too. Right, Meredith?" When she didn't answer, he looked intently into her face, reading her expression. After a moment he shook his head and exhaled gustily. "Oh, Merry Forrest, what am I going to do with you?"

Meredith shrugged. "You're going to teach me how to ride a bike. You're going to introduce me to all that carefree childhood fun you think I've missed."

"Right," Brandt said briskly. "So let's go get started."

"YOU PROMISED I'd enjoy this." Meredith was huffing painfully as she pumped away on the balky balloon-tired bike. Shaking her head to toss back the long damp strands of hair that had fallen into her face, she tried to blink away the sweat that fogged her glasses and stung her eyes. She was afraid to let go of the handlebar to wipe her forehead. "Confound you, Brandt Dahlberg," she accused fractiously, "you told me riding a bicycle would be fun. You lied."

At her side Brandt cruised leisurely on his sleek ten-speed, his feet turning the pedals without visible effort. His hair was unruffled, and the collar of his dress shirt looked as crisp as it had when he donned it in his office dressing room after showering that morning.

The two bicycles crept along the narrow ribbon of pavement that wound through the woods along the levee of the American River. Studying Meredith's tense form, Brandt suggested, "I think you'd feel better if you'd relax a little. You're clutching the handlebars so tightly I can see the muscles in your arm knotted clear up to your shoulder."

Through clenched teeth Meredith responded impatiently, "If I loosen my grip, the bike wobbles."

"It wouldn't if you'd speed up a little. As I tried to explain earlier, the wheels of a bicycle are gyroscopes, and the faster they rotate, the steadier the bike stays. It's a law of physics. Angular momentum—"

Meredith's oath was brief and pungent.

Brandt laughed. "Come on, darling, give yourself a chance. You're doing beautifully. But you have to ease into it, limber up the same way you'd warm your vocal cords before singing. In fact, you might find it easier if you did sing—"

"Sing?" she echoed, incredulous.

"Yes. It'd take your mind off the work you're doing and help you pedal in rhythm. I always hum when I'm racing."

Meredith glanced at Brandt suspiciously to see if he was teasing, but he appeared perfectly serious. The idea did make a certain amount of sense, she admitted. "And do you have any particular hits you like to sing?"

Brandt gestured airily. "Well, for short rides I favor the classics. Beethoven's *Ninth* is always good; the 'Ode to Joy' has a nice driving 4/4 beat." In a rusty baritone he began to drone.

"You're impossible," Meredith said with a giggle, but as she joined Brandt in the familiar melody, she felt her muscles loosen and her feet begin to pump in time to the music. The bike moved faster, creating a breeze that dried the sweat on her forehead. They entered the woods and all around her the floodplain of the river was lush with foliage and flowers springing out of the rich loam: blackberry thickets starred with pink blossoms, grape vines curling up the trunks of black-barked live oak trees. Sparrows and red-crowned house finches sang among the showy yellow blooms of the elder trees. At the foot of the levee the stream gurgled frothily, swollen with the runoff of the Sierra snowpack. Suddenly Meredith felt relaxed and very happy.

They rode for several miles before Brandt reluctantly declared that it was time to head back to Warcom. Meredith protested, but Brandt was insistent, and she admitted he was probably right. No point in straining something her first time out. Besides, he promised they'd come back another day.

They rode side by side, speaking little. They were almost within sight of the Warcom lot when suddenly their amiable silence was punctured by the gleeful whoops of a trio of youngsters whose bikes emerged just ahead of them, from around a bend masked by a clump of tall, feathery wild anise. Expertly the boys skidded their back wheels as they took the curve, three abreast, so intent on their race they didn't notice the two adults headed in the opposite direction. Brandt swerved. Meredith panicked. Jerking her bicycle clear off the pavement, she tried to steer, but her tires caught in the soft dirt and stopped abruptly, unbalancing her. She landed with a clatter in the underbrush.

Instantly Brandt was at her side. "Are you all right?" he demanded anxiously. When Meredith nodded, Brandt glared after the children whose shouts were already fading in the distance. "Blasted kids, they're supposed to observe safety rules here on the trail just as if they were on a street."

"Don't worry about it," Meredith reassured him, holding out a hand. "As the saying goes, only my dignity suffered—" With Brandt's help she staggered to her feet, resettling her glasses securely on her nose. "My dignity," she repeated with a grimace, looking at the smears of dirt and green sap staining her knees, "and my slacks. I hope the cleaners know how to get plant juice out of linen."

Brandt shook his head regretfully as he pulled Meredith's bike from the anise plant and propped it on the kickstand. "I'm sorry. When I borrowed the bike, I should have taken the time to find out if Annette or one of the other women could have loaned you some sweats, too. But you're sure you're okay?"

"Well, I don't see any blood." Meredith took a step. Her knees felt unsteady, and her thighs ached. Even worse, when she moved she realized her bottom was sore where it had met the hard saddle. She hoped she'd be able to sit down the next day.

Brandt nodded and swung his long leg across the bar of his lightweight bicycle. "In that case, since there doesn't seem to be any lasting damage, do you think you can go on?"

Shaking her head firmly, Meredith said, "If it's all the same to you, I've had enough exercise for one day. I'll walk." As she started pushing the bike, she called over her shoulder, "And don't you dare tell me it's like getting back on a horse after you've been thrown!"

She had strolled only a few yards when Brandt caught up with her on foot, guiding his bike with one hand. "I hope you're not going to let one spill scare you off cycling permanently. For a first lesson, you were doing very well. You have an excellent sense of balance."

Meredith glanced at him inscrutably. "I suppose I do— at least, about some things." Tossing back her hair, she took a deep breath, drinking in the warm air. "It really is beautiful in this park," she murmured. "I had no idea. It's so peaceful."

"Here by the river you can almost forget you're surrounded by a million people," Brandt agreed. "When I ride my bike to work, sometimes I wonder if this is what Sacramento was like when John Sutter settled the place in the 1830's."

"I've always assumed he chose this site because it re- minded him of his Swiss homeland. After all, he did call it New Helvetia, or Switzerland."

Brandt shook his head ironically. "Somehow I doubt that. Sacramento's nice, but it doesn't remind me of any part of Switzerland that I ever saw."

Meredith regarded Brandt curiously. "When were you in Switzerland?"

"Oh, years ago, when I was just twenty," he replied with a dismissive shrug. "During summer vacation from col- lege I went over to take part in the Brevet. That's a mar- athon the Swiss Bicycle Association sponsors each July. One of the great amateur cycling events in the world. In a hundred miles the route crosses four major Alpine passes and climbs over sixteen thousand vertical feet."

"Wow!" Meredith breathed. "Talk about grueling . . ."

"But it's wonderful, too. Not just the thrill of riding through some of the most spectacular scenery in the world, but the camaraderie. For a week beforehand, everyone camps out in tents, training in the daytime, going to clubs at night. The day of the race, you take off at sun- rise, and crowds are already lining the streets to cheer you on. You ride through quaint little villages, where people wave from their windows, past glaciers. . . ."

Brandt's eyes grew hooded, hazy with old memories. His breath quickened as if from past exertion. "It's not a timed race," he explained distantly. "The whole point is simply to finish. I prepared for months beforehand, rid- ing every chance I could get, logging thousands of miles. Dad and Walter both thought I was crazy.

"They didn't know it, but I was beginning to have sec- ond thoughts about my promise to join them at Warcom. I hadn't said anything because I knew there'd be hell to pay; it would certainly mean the end of Dad's financing my college career. But I was beginning to think that after I finished school—on an athletic scholarship, if necessary—maybe I'd join the European professional racing circuit: Milan-San Remo, the Tour de France. . . ."

"What happened?"

Meredith's blunt question cut into Brandt's reverie. His eyes cleared, and he gazed down at her, his mouth twisted with cynical self-awareness. "What happened?" he queried wryly. "Simple. My father had a stroke and died at the age of forty-seven . . . and I grew up. I had two choices: I could keep my promise to my father, finish my education in comfort at the best schools and step into a lucrative partnership in a fast-growing industry. Or I could ride bikes for a living. Put that way, the decision was fairly easy to make."

"But you still regret it."

The soft, damning words popped from Meredith's lips before she had a chance to weigh them. Seeing the distress that flickered in the depths of his blue eyes, she wished she'd kept quiet. Impulsively she reached up and touched his face, smoothing away the frown lines that scored his tanned skin. "I'm sorry, Brandt. I had no right to say that."

He covered her hand with his own, holding her fingers against his cheek. She could feel his jaw tighten, and his mustache was silky against her hand. He said resignedly, "But you're right. I do regret it. Not all the time, but every now and then when I remember the Alpine wind in my face and the crowds." Turning his head, he pressed his lips into the center of her palm. "But, Meredith, I don't regret it now, not when I'm here with you."

The moist warmth of his mouth made her shiver with need. "Oh, Brandt."

As he nuzzled her skin, he sniffed. "That's a very sexy perfume you're wearing," he noted. "Unusual. Your hands smell like sweet licorice."

She said huskily, "I'm not wearing any perfume. It—it must be the anise I fell into. I'm covered with the stuff."

"Whatever it is, you smell delicious." As he spoke, his smile widened, tickling her sensitive palm as he kissed it one last time. He drew her hand away from his face and tucked it under his elbow. Then he deftly fitted the frames of the two bicycles together so that he could push them both while Meredith held his arm.

"I've always like licorice," he remarked cheerfully, as they headed off along the path toward Warcom.

6

"HERE ARE THE LISTINGS you asked me to take a look at." The westering sun reflected off the top of Brandt's desk as Meredith held out a thick sheaf of computer paper.

"Finished? That's great," Brandt exclaimed with a smile, glancing away from his terminal. "Thank you for staying over. I know a rush job this size is a chore, but Walter insists he needs this stuff first thing in the morning. As it is, I'll probably be here all night reviewing it. Any comments you have that I should know about?"

Meredith nodded briefly. "I've made some notes in the margins." Brandt reached for the printouts, and she dropped them into his hands, stepping back before his fingers could touch hers. Her movements seemed constricted, restrained. "If you'll excuse me, it's almost six, and I'd like to go now."

Brandt frowned. It was true they were probably the only two people left in the building, but Meredith was not usually a clock watcher. "Rehearsal tonight?" he asked, surprised at his resentment at the thought of her leaving him to go join the band.

"No. I just want to get home."

Glancing at the listings with her remarks neatly penned on the edge of the pages, he continued. "Well, if you don't have something going tonight, would you mind terribly waiting just a little longer, until I've had a chance to flip through this mess? I'd like to make sure I understand your comments, otherwise I might have to bother you at home with questions."

"I . . . guess I can stay a little longer," Meredith mumbled grudgingly.

Brandt peered narrowly at her. He liked the way the silky knit blouse she wore draped softly over the gentle swell of her breasts; the tied sash on her denim wraparound skirt emphasized the slimness of her waist. Since coming to work at Warcom she had abandoned her trim little business suits in favor of the more casual attire affected by most of the company's employees. Such a dress code was a practical policy actively espoused by Walter on the grounds that a comfortable employee was a productive one. Ironically, he and Brandt were the two people whose duties prevented them from taking advantage of this relaxed attitude.

Brandt's brow furrowed as he watched Meredith. Despite the easy fit of the clothes she wore, all day long she had seemed neither comfortable nor relaxed. She moved tightly, her pliant body unyielding. Her vivid curls were pulled away from her face and secured loosely in a clip at her nape, but she held her head inflexibly, as if hairpins stabbed her scalp.

He wondered why she was behaving with such reserve. He had thought—hoped—that their ride the evening before, with its laughter and the sharing of old dreams, had put their relationship on a newer, more intimate footing. Instead, whenever he came near her, she retreated.

"Meredith," he asked, his voice deep and troubled as he searched her face, "are you all right? You seem . . . aloof."

Her hazel eyes were oddly opaque. "I'm sorry." She hunched her shoulders in an approximation of a shrug, and all at once Brandt realized he could almost count the individual freckles spattering her white skin.

"Are you sure you're feeling okay? Do you have a head-ache? You look very pale."

Meredith wet her lips. "Well," she admitted reluctantly, "I could use some aspirins. That's one of the reasons I wanted to head home. I thought I had some tablets in my purse, but—"

"Good grief, why didn't you say so sooner?" Brandt looked impatient. "In my bathroom there are aspirins and cold capsules or anything else you may need. Help your-self."

"Thank you. I didn't want to intrude." With a wan smile she turned away, still moving rigidly. Brandt watched her retreat until she passed his trophy case and disappeared through the door into his private dressing room. He tried to remember whether he'd thought to put his soiled clothes in the laundry hamper.

He heard the metallic creak of the medicine cabinet door, followed a moment later by the gush of water from the tap. Next there was a scuffling noise and the hollow glassy thud of a small bottle bouncing on the vinyl floor. Then he heard a muffled groan.

Leaping to his feet, Brandt crossed the width of his office in two long strides. He discovered Meredith doubled over, clutching the rim of the sink to balance herself while she stooped to pick up the aspirin bottle that lay unbroken at her feet. Each motion looked slow and clumsy and painful. And as she bent down, the hem of her skirt rode up, exposing the backs of her thighs almost to her hips. With dismay Brandt spotted the large angry bruise purpling her skin just above one knee.

Swooping down, he snatched the bottle out of her fingers and placed it on the counter. Then he caught her shoulders and pulled her upright. He felt her trembling as she collapsed against his chest. "All right, Meredith," he demanded, "what the hell's wrong?"

"I dropped the aspirins."

"Forget the aspirins! I mean, what have you done to yourself? What's wrong with your leg?"

"It's nothing, really," she protested, her reedy words muffled against the front of his shirt. "I'm still a little stiff from our ride, that's all."

Brandt's arms closed gently about her. He countered grimly, "No, that's not all. I saw that black-and-blue mark. You got banged up when those kids knocked you off your bike, didn't you?"

"A bit, I suppose," she conceded reluctantly. "But truly, it's not as bad as it looks. This skin of mine tends to bruise from the slightest touch. I'm used to it. Half the time I can't even recall what caused the injury."

"But you must remember landing in the anise yesterday. Why didn't you say something at the time?"

"I really thought I was okay. I felt okay. It was only when I woke up this morning that I—" She broke off abruptly.

"That you what?" Brandt prompted. He caught her chin in his fingertips, but when he tried to lift her face away from his shirtfront so that he could see her eyes, she cringed. "Please, Meredith," he urged.

Sniffling, she twisted her head in denial. Then all at once she wailed, "Oh, Brandt, I feel so awful! Every muscle in my body aches. My bottom is so sore I can't bear to sit down, my arms feel like rubber bands, and my legs... Brandt Dahlberg, don't you *dare* laugh at me!"

Relief flooded through him. He threw back his head and crowed.

"Damn it," she cried indignantly, trying to squirm from his arms, "you wouldn't think it was so funny if you were the one."

With difficulty he squelched his yelps of amusement. He gasped, "Darling, darling, I'm not laughing at you, I'm laughing because I'm happy. I thought you were behaving so strangely because I'd offended you somehow." Soothingly he nudged her back into his embrace. "I thought you were mad at me."

Meredith leaned her cheek against his chest once more. She could hear his heart beneath her ear. "I'm mad at myself," she admitted grumpily. "I feel like an idiot. As if it wasn't bad enough to be reminded that six-year-olds learn to ride bikes every day, after you talked blithely about racing a hundred miles up the side of an Alp. Then I try to log a few lousy miles on level ground and end up hurting so much I want to die...."

"Poor baby. It's all my fault. I shouldn't have coerced you into going with me. You must think I'm a tyrant."

"Absolutely merciless," Meredith agreed.

He held her cradled against him for several moments, silently stroking her hair; it was soft and silky, scented with her elusive fragrance, as enticing as her flesh. His hand encountered the clip at her nape, and realizing it was coming undone, he removed the barrette completely. He began to comb her loosened locks with his fingers, arranging the glossy tresses in a flame-bright spray down her back. When he accidentally brushed her shoulder, she flinched.

With clinical care Brandt touched her again, gingerly prodding her shoulders and back through the fabric of her blouse. Beneath her smooth skin the muscles felt knotted and strained, cramped. "Good Lord, you really are in a mess, aren't you?" he muttered grimly.

"You mustn't blame yourself," Meredith countered. "I don't think it was so much the unaccustomed exercise as it was the tension yesterday. What with the party and the singing and all, I was really keyed up."

"Whatever the reason, if we don't find a way to work this stiffness out of you now, by tomorrow you'll be worse off than ever. I doubt you'll be able to work. I'll be surprised if you can walk."

"What do you suggest?"

Catching her arms lightly, he eased her away from him so that he could search her face. His blue eyes were intent as he asked soberly, "Meredith, do you trust me?"

Her brows lifted. "Well, I thought I did . . . only there's something about the question 'Do you trust me?' that always arouses my suspicions." She grinned.

Brandt huffed and started to hug her, but thought better of it. Instead, he drawled, "I certainly hope you do trust me, because what I want you to do is take off all your clothes."

Meredith choked. "In the *office*?"

"It's well after five," he pointed out. "And we're not on company time."

"That's a relief. For a moment there I was afraid I was going to have to list you on my time card."

Laughing, Brandt released her. He swung open the door to the medicine cabinet and pulled out a bottle of milky lotion. When he uncapped it to sniff experimentally, the small bathroom was suddenly filled with the pronounced odor of wintergreen. Brandt nodded in approval and replaced the lid.

"I want you to use my shower," he instructed. "A whirlpool bath would be better, but that's one of the few luxuries Warcom doesn't provide for its employees. Start the shower going as hot and hard as you can stand it, then stay under the water for about ten minutes. When you get out, you'll find towels in the cabinet and a robe hanging behind the door. Put on the robe and come out into my office. I'm going to give you a rubdown."

Meredith gazed at Brandt. She thought of those long sinewy fingers and callused palms grazing her skin. "A rubdown?" she echoed.

"It certainly beats your suffering for the rest of the week, especially when it's my fault you're in this fix in the first place."

Her expression was candid. Both of them knew what they were inviting. "All right."

"Good." Brandt waved in the direction of the shower stall. "Now get the water going. It looks as if we'll miss dinner while you soak, so I'll run down to the cafeteria and see if I can forage a couple of sandwiches." He pivoted on his heel and left, closing the door behind him.

She waited for a count of twenty-five, until she was confident Brandt was out of the office. Reaching for the tie on the waistband of her denim skirt, she caught her image in the mirror over the sink and paused, suddenly unaccountably shy.

Meredith had never been in this room before, preferring instead to tend her own needs in the women's lounge across the corridor from her office. Brandt's hairbrush lay on the counter, a golden strand caught in the bristles; the scent of his after-shave lingered in the air. The closet door was ajar, and she could see a row of starchy dress shirts on hangers. This was Brandt's inner sanctum, where he came alone to wash away the sweat of his morning rides and don the sophisticated suits he wore for work. His was the only form that ever reflected off the chrome fixtures, the only body that dripped on the utilitarian white bath mat. Simply being here seemed an invasion of his privacy, and to

disrobe in front of his mirrors seemed to Meredith akin to
doing a striptease.

She glanced toward the medicine cabinet. Perhaps she
should just take two aspirins and go home, pleading a
headache. Surely her soreness would be better by morning. But as soon as the thought formed, she rejected it.
Brandt had said she needed a massage and he was a trained
athlete, experienced in sports medicine. Besides, Meredith admitted, jerking loose the bow that held her skirt in
place, there was no way she was going to pass up an opportunity to feel his hands on her body again.

The needles of scalding water gushing from the spigot
made such a racket on the pebbled-glass walls of the
shower stall that Meredith did not hear Brandt return to
his office. She was relishing the sting of the spray against
her naked skin, the near-cutting force of individual
streams lancing her sore muscles. The air inside the cu-
bicle was hot and steamy, and with each deep breath she
seemed to inhale some tropical balm that numbed her
senses. Rotating slowly under the shower head, she could
feel herself relaxing, growing languid.

Knuckles rapped insistently on the bathroom door.
"Meredith, you've been in there forever! It's time to get
out."

Rousing herself, she reluctantly turned the handles
clockwise. The water slowed to a dribble and stopped. She
pushed open the door of the shower stall and stepped out
onto the bath mat, shivering violently as chill air hit her.
The water streaming from her wet hair felt like ice. She
found a towel and wrapped it in a turban around her head.

"Meredith!" Even muffled by the thickness of the door
and the heavy white terry dressing gown draped over a
hook on the back of it, she could hear the impatience in
his voice.

"Coming, I'm coming," she called back. She grabbed for her glasses, but the humid atmosphere in the bathroom had clouded the lenses with steam; if she tried to wipe them dry, she knew the moist air would only fog them again.

Setting down the glasses, she reached for the robe and slipped into it. It was far too large for her, dragging around her ankles, weighing down her shoulders. The sleeves hung past her fingertips. Folding back the cuffs, she struggled with the bulky cloth belt to cinch it around her waist. The wide lapels gaped open. Arranging the folds of fabric around her, Meredith realized it was saturated with the smell of Brandt. Where the plush material brushed across her naked breast, it felt like his caressing hand.

When she emerged from the bathroom, taking tiny cautious steps to avoid tripping on the robe as she fumbled blindly across the room, Brandt gaped. Until that moment he had not quite appreciated what a lovely face she had. But with her body hidden beneath the shapeless dressing gown, her vivid hair masked behind a white towel, her features were thrown into new prominence. For some reason she was clutching her glasses in her hand instead of wearing them, and without the oversize frames he could see the delicate, clean-boned line of her jaw, the wide hazel eyes starred with red-gold lashes. Her complexion was exquisite. Washed free of cosmetics, flushed and dewy from the hot shower, her skin was not freckled and pale as she described it but a translucent shell, pink dappled with gold, like the throat of a lily. He hated the idea that insensitive clods had made her deprecate her looks simply because they were unique.

Meredith cleared her throat, and Brandt realized he'd been staring. "Sorry," he muttered, abashed. Indicating the plastic-wrapped containers on his desk, he said, "The best I could find in the cafeteria was tuna or ham sand-

wiches or peanut butter and jelly. Since I didn't know
which you preferred, I chose the tuna and ham. Also some
cole slaw. There's potato salad if—" Conscious he was
babbling, Brandt abruptly stopped talking. He forced his
mouth into a strained smile. "Would you prefer to eat first,
or shall we go ahead with the rubdown?"

"I'm not very hungry," Meredith replied.

Brandt let out his breath with a hiss. "Okay." He pointed
to the sofa, over which he had spread several bath towels.
He picked up the bottle of lotion. "If you'll just lie face
down . . ."

She placed her glasses on the end table. Squinting, she
asked dubiously, "I don't have to take the robe off, do I?"

He shook his head. "No. I'll work around it."

The sofa seat was wide and long, and very comfortable. Stretching out on the towels, Meredith cradled her
cheek on her crossed arms and closed her eyes. "All set,"
she murmured.

Brandt sank to his knees on the carpet beside her and
rolled back his shirt sleeves. When the smell of wintergreen tickled her nostrils, she knew he had opened the
bottle of lotion. He pushed the hem of the robe up to her
knees, baring her calves, and Meredith grew rigid, her
breathing becoming rapid.

"Come on, Meredith, don't tense up," he crooned. "The
whole point of this little exercise is to get you to unwind,
not hyperventilate. Try to take slow, steady breaths."
Obediently Meredith tempered her respiration. Fingers
captured one ankle, lifting it, and a stream of frosty liquid dripped across her instep.

"Hey, that stuff's cold," she complained, but almost at
once the spot where the lotion pooled on the bottom of her
foot began to tingle and warm. Strong thumbs smoothed
out the liquid, spreading the warmth, rubbing it into her

skin. Methodically Brandt massaged the ball of her foot, flexed each toe. As he worked the stiffness out of the muscles, Meredith heaved a delicious sigh. "Mm, that's nice. Better than a chiropodist."

"Thanks. It's good to know I have other skills I can fall back on if the bottom ever drops out of the electronics market." He trailed his fingertips over her instep.

Meredith wriggled. "Don't do that. I'm ticklish."

"Sorry." Slapping her heels lightly, Brandt moved to her calves where the tendons and muscles were almost visibly stressed. Prodding the balled hamstring experimentally, he felt her shrink from him. At once he softened his touch. Feathering his fingertips in subtle circles, he moved upward along the curve of her leg, until her breath quickened and she shifted beneath his hand. Deliberately he stroked the potently erogenous flesh at the back of her knee. Meredith gasped.

"Am I hurting you?"

Her mouth muffled in her arms, Meredith mumbled languidly, "No—oh, no. This feels very relaxing, very... good." *Talk about understatements*, she thought with drowsy irony. The sweet pain of his fingers mapping the taut muscles of her out-of-shape body was incredibly erotic. Far beyond merely helping her to relax, Brandt's clever hands had left her boneless, lissome and pliant. Acquiescent. She would give him anything he asked, as long as he did not stop touching her.

She felt the hem of the robe being pushed still higher, until it lay draped across her buttocks, preserving the last vestiges of her modesty. Brandt poured more lotion into his cupped palm, warming it between his hands. Minty fumes rose in a cloying cloud, combining with the musky smell of the leather upholstery into a heady, pervasive perfume Meredith found almost narcotic.

With sure, even movements Brandt began rubbing the liquid into her thighs. When his fingers reached the ugly black-and-purple blotch above her knee, he paused. "That's a deep bruise," he observed. "Are you sure you aren't really hurt? Maybe you fractured something."

"I'm sure. I'm one of those people who can't bump into a door without looking as if I've been in a three-car pile-up. I think the condition's genetic or something. My mother was the same way. Of course," Meredith added with a yawn, "my mom was one of those clear-skinned redheads with a complexion like magnolia petals. I always envied her that."

Brandt stared at the long slim legs lying exposed to his gaze, the sleek calves and thighs curving upward into a pert bottom only partly hidden by the terry robe. She looked sweet and succulent. He wondered what would happen if he kissed her there. "Meredith," he said thickly, "you have no reason to be envious of anyone. Your skin is beautiful. I love to look at it. I . . . love to touch it."

Meredith raised her head. Kneeling beside the sofa, Brandt's face was only inches from hers, and even without her glasses she could see the naked hunger in his eyes. "I love for you to touch me," she murmured, lifting herself on one elbow. She tugged the sash knot free and the bulky dressing gown slipped off her shoulders and fell to her waist.

Her breasts were not large, but they were high and well-shaped, rising to rosebud crests already crinkled in invitation. Brandt studied her reverently. "Oh, Merry Forrest." He was almost too awed to move.

She caught his fingers in her own and guided his hand to her breast, pressing the nipple tenderly into his rough palm. Brandt trembled. His tongue flicked across his dry lips, and his breath was warm on her skin as he leaned closer. Closing her eyes, she threw back her head and offered him the slope of her throat. He began to caress her with his mouth, tiny sipping kisses that tingled and trailed over the hollows above her collarbone.

"I really do love for you to touch me," she repeated, sighing. "I really do love—" His mouth covered hers.

By the time his lips left hers, she was too languid even to open her eyes. Melting onto the couch, she waited in drowsy anticipation as clever hands pushed aside the lapels of the robe, baring all of her body. The whisper of a shirt drifting to the floor, the faint rasp of a sliding zipper were like sound effects in a dream. The mustache tickling her breasts, her navel, her thighs was a butterfly against her skin.

Meredith shivered and Brandt jerked back as if scalded. "I'm sorry!" he cried.

Her eyes were glazed as she stared up into his face. "Sorry for what?"

His voice was husky and contrite. "I didn't mean to hurt you."

"You didn't hurt me."

"Are you sure? I kissed you near the bruise, and you flinched. I was afraid—"

Meredith's lips curved tenderly. "That wonderful mouth, those hands could never hurt me, darling. If I seemed to react violently, it's because every time you touch me anywhere, you have a rather devastating effect on me."

"No more than you have on me," Brandt groaned. "Look at me, Meredith. Please."

Reluctantly she lifted her head. He was still kneeling beside the sofa, the wonderful body she'd loved in shorts and T-shirt even more impressive nude. She laid her palm on his chest, pressing it into the taut, tanned skin with its fine sprinkling of almost white hair. She could feel his heart thud.

"You see?" he said, a catch in his voice. "Lay one finger on me and my blood pressure goes shooting right through the top of my skull. It's probably just as well that all those years of cycling have left me in pretty good condition."

Meredith's own heart was racing so fast she thought she might faint. "Pretty good?" She tried unsuccessfully to match his insouciant tones. "Is that all you think you are? You're not just pretty good, you're fantastic. Gorgeous. In fact, that first day we met, when I went to help you up after you fell off your bike—"

"You mean when you tried to run me down in that van?"

"When you fell off your bike," she repeated emphatically, "and I saw you lying on the asphalt, all I could think of was what a tragedy it would have been if such a beautiful body had been damaged."

"Am I to assume from that statement that if I'd been flabby and balding, you would have considered it open season?" Brandt chided.

"It's not funny!" she protested, inexplicably hurt by his humor.

Her hazel eyes looked oddly vulnerable in her gold-dappled face, and for some reason Brandt remembered what she had told him about her girlhood, about being forced to confront audiences of hostile, mocking strangers. Did she have the idea that he was somehow jeering her performance now?

"Sweetheart, I'm not laughing at you," he told her urgently. "I've never been more serious in my life. I want you. If I crack stupid jokes, it's only because knowing you want me in return makes me feel giddy." His voice was throaty. "You make me feel more aroused than I've ever been in my life." He paused, watching her. "Please, Meredith, don't be afraid to touch me. Feel my need for you."

Her fingers drifted downward, raking through the soft hair that arrowed from his chest to his flat stomach, circling his navel to his loins with their thatch of coarser dark-blond curls. "Like this?" she whispered, finding his strength, holding him. "Is this what you want?"

He groaned. "You'll never know how much."

"Yes, I will." She lay back on the cushions. "Can't you tell I'm as ready for you as you are for me?" She guided his hand to her. She was honey and spice, silk and dew-drenched roses.

"God, Meredith—"

"I need you now," she cried, clutching at him. "Oh, Brandt." She urged him onto her, glorying in his weight. Digging her fingers into the taut muscles of his flat buttocks, she pulled him closer. "It seems like I've been waiting forever." Then he was with her, in her, and the only reality was their tireless need for each other.

"I DIDN'T PLAN for it to happen this way. In the office, I mean," Brandt admitted wryly. He was stroking Meredith's hair while she lay against him, her head on his chest. She was still wearing his robe, but he had slipped on his shirt and trousers, and they sat wound together on the sofa in the twilight. "I always expected we'd go away somewhere, maybe Mendocino or Carmel."

Her reply was muffled against the front of his shirt, which had somehow become saturated with the scent of wintergreen. "Before you picked a spot, you might have told me we were going to become lovers."

"Didn't you already know?"

She sighed happily. "From the very first day we met."

He kissed the top of her head. "You're a minx, you know that?"

"If you say so. I've never been quite sure exactly what a minx is."

"Well, darling," Brandt sighed, "according to my definition, a minx is an incredibly desirable woman who tempts me to forget that I have at least three hours' worth of work waiting for me on my desk. I'd sure as hell hate to have to explain to Walter why it didn't get done!"

"Do you think he'd disapprove?" Meredith asked, frowning. Until that moment she hadn't even stopped to consider whether Warcom had some kind of policy against office romances.

Brandt chuckled. "Walter disapprove of us? No, of course not. The man's a romantic at heart. But I'm sure he'd be disappointed in my choice of locations, not to mention the fact that I didn't first court you with dinner and a dozen roses."

"You brought me a tuna sandwich," Meredith pointed out. "And anyway, Walter once told me that he thinks flowers are banal."

"Well, I prefer my gifts to be a little more traditional than Warren's balloons." Brandt paused and when he spoke again, his voice sounded deeper and oddly diffident. "Actually, sweetheart, I did bring you a present today. I wanted to give it to you this morning, but you seemed so standoffish that I never found the right moment."

"A present?" Meredith watched, puzzled, as Brandt slipped from her arms and went into the bathroom. She heard the closet door slide in its track, and a moment later he reappeared carrying a round fiberboard carton. When he gravely handed it to her, she saw that it was an old hatbox, dusty and yellow with age. "I don't understand."

"Open it, and maybe you will," Brandt suggested.

She set the box on her lap. It was not very heavy. With trembling fingers she removed the lid and peeked inside. A soft bulky object was shrouded in tissue paper so old it crumbled at her touch. Carefully, she pushed the paper aside to reveal a teddy bear.

"His name is Pooh," Brandt said gruffly. "Not the most original name, but there was a time when he was my best friend in the world."

Meredith gazed mistily at the toy. One button eye was missing, and a round floppy ear had pulled loose from its seam, exposing cotton batting. Large patches of brown nylon fur were rubbed away from the fabric backing, and the plush that remained was matted from much wear. Meredith thought the forlorn-looking creature was the most beautiful gift she'd ever received.

"Oh, Brandt," she whispered.

"I thought you might like to have him to keep you company when we're not together." Tenderly he watched as she stroked the stuffed toy with bemused, almost reverent delicacy. "Maybe I ought to be jealous," he joked.

"Oh, Brandt," she repeated, gazing up at him with loving eyes. She caught his hand and held it against her cheek. "You'll never know—"

"Yes, I do." His fingers curled along the curve of her jaw. When her lips pressed into his palm, he groaned thickly. "Meredith, let's get away, just the two of us."

"I'd like that," she agreed simply.

Brandt sank onto the couch beside her again. "Now all we have to do is figure out where and when." His body reacting to her nearness, he continued with some difficulty, "I suspect when should be as soon as possible. As to where . . ." His tone became sly. "I mentioned Carmel. We could always borrow a bicycle for you and ride along the coast at Big Sur."

Meredith shifted restlessly on her tender bottom. Now that the afterglow of their lovemaking was fading, her body was reminding her forcefully of her various aches and pains. "Not today, please!"

"Not even if we bring a nice fluffy pillow for you to sit on?"

She clutched the teddy bear to her breast as if it was a shield. "Not even if you bring me a whole feather bed!"

Brandt hugged her bracingly. "Poor baby, I'm sorry. I shouldn't tease. But I do think you'll enjoy cycling, once you've had a little more experience." He fell silent for a moment. Then, surprisingly, he asked, "By the way, can you handle a car with a standard transmission?"

"Uh-huh. My Toyota has a stick shift. Why do you ask?"

He looked slightly ill at ease. "Well, because I need someone to drive my Volvo for me Saturday. If it weren't for the fact that the annual northern California double-century race is on, we could go away this weekend. But I ride in this race every year. It's quite an event. The course goes from the town of Davis up into the mountains around Lake Berryessa and then back down through the wine country of the Napa Valley—"

"That's a long way!"

"Two hundred miles. That's what 'double century' means. Anyway, I need someone who'll go along in my sag wagon, the support car that carries food, water, replacement tires, first-aid equipment, anything I may need along the route. Annette Nakatani's son has done it for me in the past, but the other day he was given tickets to a rock concert in San Francisco, so now I need to locate a new driver." Brandt grinned engagingly. "You'd be doing me a big favor, and it would give you a chance to observe serious cycling firsthand."

She hesitated, remembering the recording session Mike's band had scheduled for the following Sunday. "It depends. How long does this race last?"

Brandt shrugged. "Well, it starts about daylight Saturday morning, and riders have up to twenty-four hours to complete the circuit. The winners usually make it back to Davis in eight or nine hours. Since I participate more or less just to stay in practice, it'll probably take me about twelve hours to finish."

"Only twelve hours to ride two hundred miles through the mountains?"

"These mountains are hardly the Alps, you know! Barring disasters, we can be back to Davis before nightfall. There's usually some kind of party going on, which would give you a chance to meet other cyclists from the area. Or, if you prefer, we could come home fairly early in the evening."

His home, just the two of them. Meredith smiled provocatively. "But after a ride like that, are you going to be in any condition to take proper advantage of what's left of the night?"

"I'll do my best." He reached across to brush his fingertips over her breast. "Please, love," he urged, "you'd really be helping me out, and it would give us a chance to be with each other, even if you are in a car and I'm on a ten-speed. I know this isn't exactly what we had in mind for our weekend away from it all, but you'd be sharing in something that's very important to me. Who knows? Maybe someday you'll ride the race alongside me."

"Maybe." Meredith wriggled closer, drowsy and content, clutching the teddy bear in her arms. "Yes, I think I'd like that," she said more firmly. When Brandt had given her the toy, he had offered her a glimpse of his past, serene and secure as hers had never been. Now he called up tan-

talizing visions of the two of them enjoying a future together—visions too entrancing to deny.

"I'M GOING TO BE OUT of town all day Saturday," Meredith informed her brother as she switched on the steam
iron and began to press her work clothes.

Mike, hunched over the dining room table, marking
notes on music manuscript paper, glanced up, a question
in his hazel eyes. "You and the jock going somewhere?"

"Uh-huh," Meredith responded. She described her role
in the bicycle race.

"Sounds tiring," Mike commented. "I hope you don't
wear yourself out so you can't sing. You haven't forgotten, have you, that we're taping Sunday afternoon?"

"Since I'm helping foot the bill for the studio," she rejoined, "it's highly unlikely that I will forget. And don't
worry, I won't wear myself out. I plan to be at the recording session all chipper and in good voice."

"Do you plan to spend the night with your jock?"

Meredith met his gaze steadily. "Probably."

With a sigh Mike laid down his pen and rubbed the back
of his neck. His Byronic face was troubled. "Merry, hon,"
he began, "I know it's a little late in life for me to start behaving like an autocratic big brother—"

"Then don't."

He shook his head. "But I have to. I'm really worried
about you. Do you have any idea how deeply you're getting involved with this guy? I'm not talking about the fact
that you want to go to bed with him. Hey, you're an
adult—"

"Watch it, Mike," Meredith warned, not looking up
from the skirt she had been pleating. "You're getting of-
fensive."

"I'm sorry. I don't want to offend you, sis, I just want to understand. Since we were kids we've known exactly what we wanted out of life, what our goals were . . . as individuals and as a family. Music was everything. All we've ever done has been aimed at achieving those goals. And now you seem to want to throw away everything for some guy who can't even play an instrument."

"Brandt appreciates good music. He's really quite knowledgeable about classic jazz."

"A dilettante," Mike dismissed.

"At least he's not tone deaf." Meredith set the iron on end and crossed the room to her brother's side. Patting him on the shoulder, she said gently, "Mike, I love you and I know you love me. I know you're concerned about me. But let's just ease up on each other, okay? I don't want to fight with you."

She glanced past him to the manuscript pages scattered across the table, the staffs filled in with Mike's distinctive notation. "Are you working up new charts for the group?" she asked.

He shook his head. "A couple more car dealers have asked me for jingles. The pay is only so-so, but I figured you'd appreciate some help with expenses."

"Money is always nice," Meredith agreed, picking up a sheet. She scanned the page curiously. It was apparently a part written for a solo instrument, some sweet, bluesy tune she did not recognize. "What's this? It doesn't sound like a commercial."

Mike shrugged. "It's a little something of my own. May I have it back, please?"

Meredith held the page out of his reach. *Melody for C*, he had scrawled above the top staff. She might have dismissed the title as a grammatical error, except that the melody was not in the key of C but in F. Frowning, she noticed something else. "What instrument is this written for? None of our guys play in this range."

Half rising, Mike snatched the paper from her hands. "It's for piccolo," he muttered.

"Piccolo?" Meredith stared. "Who on earth do you know who plays jazz piccolo?"

Mike only blushed.

7

MEREDITH WAS TIRED. She'd been up since four o'clock that morning, and now it was afternoon. She sat on the hood of the Volvo, one in a string of support cars parked along the shoulder of the highway near the race's hundred-mile checkpoint. Rubbing the bridge of her nose under her sunglasses, she debated which was more exhausting: riding the route on a bicycle, or fighting the massive traffic jam that followed the pack.

The last time Brandt had stopped to wolf a granola bar, washed down by a quart of cold water, he had told Meredith delightedly that everything was going well. He told her he was making better time than he had in years and that she might as well drive ahead to the checkpoint and wait for him there.

Meredith was glad he was still enjoying himself. She had already seen several other support crews loading bicycles onto carrying racks, while the defeated riders sat glumly on the ground beside the cars. Their disconsolate expressions were heartbreaking. She hoped they felt better once they'd rested. Personally, all she wanted to do was take a nap.

The day had started well, if obscenely early. Brandt's soft knock on her door had come before five o'clock. When Meredith crept out of her apartment into the pearly predawn darkness, she found him waiting tensely for her. His rangy body was garbed in a bright jersey and European cycling shorts that displayed the heavy muscles of his thighs, hard sinewy legs sprinkled with fine sun-bleached hair. White socks emphasized his tan. He looked sleek, powerful, devastatingly potent. Brandt was a handsome man no matter what he wore, but athletic gear suited him best, reinforcing the impression of latent strength he created.

"You're looking lean and mean this morning," Meredith had commented appreciatively, puzzled by his vaguely distracted air. She had expected a more passionate greeting. When Brandt bent down to brush his lips across hers, she realized he was trembling with leashed energy. That was why he seemed only marginally aware of her presence—he was already psyching himself up for the race.

They ate breakfast in an all-night coffee shop, where Meredith sipped her coffee and watched in awe as Brandt plowed through stack after stack of pancakes with syrup. The ravenous display disturbed her. Carefully she queried, "Should you really be eating so much right before the race? Won't a full stomach make you sick?"

Brandt glanced up, suddenly aware of his preoccupied silence, his questionable table manners. Smiling sheepishly, he wiped his mouth and explained, "Sorry, Meredith, you must think I'm acting like a pig. Usually I'm a coffee and juice man, but right now I have to force carbohydrates, for energy. I've been doing it for a couple of days, to prepare for the race. The drain on my body's reserves will be phenomenal. Even after shoveling in the pasta and bread for three days, I know that by the last fifty miles, it's all going to be gone. It's like hitting the wall that marathon runners talk about. From that point on, every calorie of energy I expend will actually deplete my body."

"Good Lord," Meredith breathed. "Why should you or anyone else want to put yourself through all that? Surely not just for a trophy."

Brandt said, "Actually, very few of the participants are trying for the trophy. Most of them, like me, do it because they think it's fun."

"Fun?"

Brandt shrugged. "Well, regardless of his elapsed time, everyone who completes the circuit does get a jacket patch."

Meredith shook her head in exasperation. "And how many patches do you have?"

"Eleven," Brandt said blithely. "It should have been twelve, but I missed the race the year I was married. My wife refused to drive the sag wagon. Now that I think about it, I suspect that's one of the main reasons I'm no longer married."

He saw Meredith's look of shock. Setting down his fork, he reached across the table and captured her fingers in his. He caressed her palm with his thumb as he explained, "Darling, I know what I just said makes me sound like a jerk, selfish and self-centered. That's exactly what I was, then. So was she. We were a couple of spoiled, immature kids who had no business whatsoever getting married. In retrospect I'm surprised we stuck it out a month, much less a year."

"You weren't in love with her?" Meredith probed quietly, her irrational jealousy of Brandt's former wife superseded by the difficulty of imagining him as a callow, egocentric youth.

He shrugged. "Love didn't come into it. Cynthia was bright and pretty and willing enough at first, but our interests and goals were completely different. We thought we knew what we were doing, but it soon became obvious that beyond being compatible lovers, we had nothing in common. Worse, we had no particular desire to develop any common interests.

"In retrospect, I'm ashamed to say that the driving force behind my proposal must have been the secret thought— or perhaps the hope—that Walter would disapprove. Which he did. No matter how fond I was of the man, in my heart I resented abandoning my so-called career as a professional cyclist. I was determined to show Walter that even though he and my late father might have 'trapped' me into working at Warcom, I was still in charge of my private life.

"Unfortunately, what I didn't realize was that I was also trying to be in charge of Cynthia's life, trying to squelch her ambitions and mold her the same way my dad had tried to mold me. All I succeeded in doing was making her miserable. Finally she said to hell with me and took off."

Brandt shook his head. "At least it ended without too many permanent scars. Cynthia and her second husband run a dancing school in Seattle. They send me a card every Christmas." Squeezing Meredith's hand, he changed the subject.

For the rest of the meal, and during the twenty-mile drive to the college town of Davis, Brandt filled her in on details of the race. It was dawn when he parked the Volvo near the campus of the University of California.

While Brandt changed into his cleated cycling shoes and did some stretching exercises, Meredith removed his bike from the carrying rack on the bumper. The bicycle he was riding in the event was not the one on which he commuted to work, the one Meredith had struck with Mike's van. This was a state-of-the-art racing model, with silk sew-up tires and a titanium frame so light she could lift it with one hand.

When Meredith admired it, Brandt dismissed her comment with a bland, "Yes, it is nice, isn't it?" But later, as they waited in line to have his control card stamped, a teenage couple with three-speed touring bikes came up to greet Brandt. Meredith overheard them estimate his racer's value and she was flabbergasted.

"Next year you'll have to ride with me," Brandt whispered, his mouth hard on hers as he kissed her for luck.

"Yes," she said huskily. Another rider called Brandt's name, and Meredith felt rather forlorn as she moved away from him to join the spectators lined along the shoulder of the road. It seemed to her that the cyclists were going to have all the fun.

To her surprise, however, the people in the crowd were as friendly and outgoing as the racers. A very pregnant woman wearing a jacket covered with patches introduced herself and exclaimed, "This is your first race? That's great!" Patting her belly, she laughed. "I've always ridden with my husband in the past, but as you can see, that's not an option this year. But let me tell you, whether you're on a bike or in a car, there's no race like the first one." Other people standing around echoed her comments, and Meredith recalled what Brandt had told her about the camaraderie shared by the participants in that Swiss bicycle race. She began to take more interest in what was going on. By the time the starting pistol cracked, she was as excited as the other onlookers were.

The shot of the gun was followed by a cheer from the crowd. Cyclists of all ages on bicycles of every possible description filed across the line, headed westward toward the low mountain range that separated California's central valley from the Pacific coast beyond.

The air hummed with the metallic whir of chains on sprockets, gears clicking. Meredith watched Brandt pass, standing in the pedals, his body almost horizontal as he bent over the handlebars and downstroked in a slow, deliberate rhythm, warming and stretching his muscles. Although his expression was partially obscured by his perforated plastic safety helmet, his jaw was clenched and he looked determined. Meredith waved, but she was certain he would not see her. When he lifted his head to smile in her direction, her heart flipped. Then he was gone.

As the clump of racers disappeared into the distance, the pregnant woman patted Meredith's shoulder and laughed. "Well, honey, looks like it's time for us to get to work. Drive carefully. If we don't bump into each other again today, then I'll see you next year—hopefully on a bike!" Meredith said goodbye and returned to the Volvo.

For Brandt the race was now half over. All day long he had ridden, sprinting on the flatlands, downshifting when he hit the grade leading up into the mountains. He circled the long rugged shoreline of Lake Berryessa, a large reservoir several thousand feet above sea level, its shimmering surface dotted with houseboats and fishermen in canoes. His ride had gone smoothly so far, without incident beyond changing a bent spoke.

Meredith was grateful for that. The checkpoints doubled as first-aid stations, and passing a couple of them, she had spotted riders being treated for cuts and abrasions. At one station, paramedics were loading a man with a broken leg into an ambulance. His bicycle lay twisted and crumpled beside the road.

Thus far Brandt had ridden without spilling, and he would cross this checkpoint behind those riders seriously competing for the trophy, but still far ahead of the majority of the pack. The difficult part of the course would be behind him. He had another hundred miles to go, winding out of the mountains and through the vineyards of the

Napa Valley before heading eastward back to Davis, but from this point on the route was almost all downhill.

Sitting on the edge of the Volvo's hood, her denim-clad legs dangling, Meredith kicked her feet back and forth feeling like a child. Even in the mountains the direct sun was surprisingly hot, making her grateful for the cool sleeveless tank top she wore. The torpid pine-perfumed air was soporific.

Along the graveled shoulder of the road a line of sag wagons was parked, their occupants similarly killing time. In the car next to the Volvo, a boy in a college sweatshirt was setting out buckets of iced soft drinks. Spotting Meredith, he wandered to her side and offered her one.

At first she hesitated, but realized her caution was unnecessary when he noted, "You're with Brandt Dahlberg, aren't you?"

She nodded, and the boy said approvingly, "He's a good rider, especially for someone his age. I drive support for my fraternity brothers—I'm into swimming, myself—and every year Dahlberg manages to beat most of the guys." Ignoring his youthful conceit, Meredith chatted with him easily until at last Brandt appeared over the rise.

The instant she spotted him, Meredith bade the boy a hasty goodbye and ran back to the Volvo. Brandt's head was bent so low he seemed to be resting his chin on the handlebars. Sometime since she'd last seen him he had stripped off his jersey and tied it like a sash around his waist, leaving his broad shoulders bare, muscles rippling in the sunshine. His bronzed skin was dusted with a faint powdering of salty dried sweat like the bloom on a grape.

He braked to a halt at the checkpoint, pausing long enough for the monitor to stamp his control card and mark his name on a list. Scanning the row of cars, he finally spotted Meredith waving beside the Volvo. When he pedaled slowly along the edge of the pavement to reach her, his bike wobbled noticeably.

"You're right, I must be a masochist," he croaked, half falling off the bicycle, though catching it before the frame could hit the gravel. Brandt sprawled against the side of the car, his breathing hoarse and labored. Wordlessly, Meredith handed over a plastic squirt bottle of water, and he aimed a long stream directly into his parched throat, gulping greedily. Some of the liquid overflowed the sides of his mouth and dribbled down his jaw. "More," he gasped. Meredith started to refill the bottle from a gallon jug. Ripping off his helmet, Brandt grabbed the jug from her hands and poured the water directly onto his head.

Water gushed over him, flowing from his sodden hair onto his forehead, his nose, beading on his mustache before it dripped over his chin and ran in rivulets down his hard throat onto the heavy muscles of his shoulders. Meredith followed each drop as it dredged its way through the salt coating his skin to at last become entangled in the hair on his heaving chest. He had dug his cleated shoes into the gravel in order to prop himself against the side of the car and his thighs twitched. His cycling shorts, blotched with patches of sweat, clung to him revealingly. Meredith turned away and began rummaging through the foam cooler for something for him to eat.

His exhaustion disturbed her; he looked completely wiped out. The contrast to his exuberant confidence at the last stop was almost shocking. She wondered if he had hit that wall he talked about sooner than he'd expected.

With shaking fingers he accepted the apple she offered, and after that for several minutes the only sound between them was the crunch of his teeth biting into the fruit's crisp red skin. By the time he finished the snack, he had perked up a little. Tossing the core into a litter bag, he untied his discarded jersey from around his waist and started to wipe his mouth with one of the sleeves. At the rank odor of the fabric, he grimaced and used the back of his glove instead.

"Meredith, would you please get me a clean shirt?" he asked, his voice stronger than it had been. "There are a couple of spares in the back seat of the car. And while you're at it, I could use the liniment as well."

She watched as he tugged on a cotton T-shirt she'd found, and then uncapped the familiar wintergreen lotion. "Damned knees are always the first things to go," he grumbled as he stripped off his gloves and began to rub the cream into his calves and kneecaps.

"Would you like me to do that for you?" she asked, remembering the feel of his hands on her own body.

He shook his head. "No, thanks, love. I can do it faster, and I really do need to get back on the road. We're only halfway home, you know."

"Are you sure you're up to finishing the race?" she asked hesitantly, worried yet not wanting to dampen his confidence.

He reached for his gloves and helmet. "Of course I'm up to it," he insisted.

Meredith touched his arm, stilling him. She could feel the tremor in his hard muscles. "Shouldn't you wait a while longer before going on? I think you ought to rest more."

Glancing toward the road, Brandt hesitated. "Darling, I'm just fine. I do this every year."

"Please, Brandt. For me."

Because of her sunglasses, he couldn't see her eyes, but her mouth was tight with concern. Brandt sighed. Smoothing her lips with his fingertips, he said, "All right, sweetheart. Whatever you want."

The sun was directly overhead, but by draping a blanket across the open car door, Meredith was able to fabricate a tiny patch of shade. Brandt spread his jersey over the gravel and urged Meredith down beside him. Leaning against the side of the car, they huddled together, her head on his shoulder as they relished the relative coolness of the makeshift tent.

He caught her hand in his and splayed her fingers across his bare thigh. Her skin was astonishingly white against his tan. "This is nice," he murmured, toying with her nails. "It's been a long time since anyone fussed over me."

His wistful statement caught Meredith off guard, making her realize how very much she still had to learn about her lover, despite their intimacy. Brandt always seemed so composed, so self-reliant, that it had never occurred to her to wonder whether he might be lonely. Poor man—divorced, family long dead—of course he was lonely. At least she'd always had her brother.

"If there's no one to fuss over you, then you must learn to take better care of yourself," she admonished with mock severity. "Take this race, for example. Exercise is one thing, but why in heaven's name would anyone deliberately set out to torture himself the way you and all the other riders do? I don't understand the attraction. Is it just an ego boost you get from being able to say you've cycled two hundred miles?"

Brandt laughed. "Oh, ego is part of it, I'm sure; the satisfaction of meeting a challenge you've set for yourself. But there's more to it than that. Sustained exertion can be very pleasurable physically, as well. After a certain point a chemical reaction takes place in the muscles that stimulates exhilaration, a genuine natural high."

"I did notice you seemed a little giddy at your last checkpoint."

"Probably I was. The high doesn't last, unfortunately, but while it does, there's nothing like it."

Meredith lifted her head. "Nothing?"

"Well, almost nothing," Brandt teased. Drawing her against him, he draped his arm over her shoulders so that his hand dangled at the low neckline of her tank top, his rough palm brushing the swell of her breast. Meredith slithered closer, and his fingers dipped inside the blouse. When they found her nipple, she shivered.

"I-I think I u-understand what you're saying," she stammered, her words roughened by the ripples of delight he was arousing. "There are moments when the act of singing can generate that kind of excitement, when the voice is perfectly tuned and the music is good and the audience is responsive. It doesn't happen very often for me, but when it all comes together in just the right way, then yes, the feeling can be very satisfying."

Brandt's hand stilled. "More satisfying than math?" he questioned darkly.

Meredith shrugged. "Not for me, it isn't. But I'd be the last person in the world to deny that occasionally show business can be very. . . seductive."

"It has that effect on some people," Brandt said, remembering Cynthia. He leaned out from under the jury-rigged canopy and looked toward the highway. A dozen riders were filing past the checkpoint. "Meredith, I'm going to have to get back on the road again."

"Just like that?" she clucked in aggrieved tones. "I will never understand athletes!"

Brandt picked up his helmet and gloves again. "You don't have to understand athletes, darling—just this one." Sweeping her into his arms, he pressed his mouth over hers in a rough, breathless kiss. "We're in this together." He jumped on his bicycle and was gone.

The Napa Valley was lush and fertile, the sheer force of its beauty enough to revive Meredith's flagging energy as she followed the racers. Banks of golden mustard edged the roadbed, their bright yellow starred with the more vivid scarlet-orange of California poppies. Flocks of birds pecked at the dark earth between the endless rows of freshly pruned grapes in the manicured vineyards. High above the valley floor two rainbow-striped hot air balloons danced on the breeze. Beneath them signs pointed to wineries in little towns with musical names like St. Helena, Calistoga, Geyserville.

As the settlements grew closer together, traffic increased, and the racers slowed and clumped. Meredith realized that she was in sight of Brandt's group once more, the Volvo cruising only a hundred yards behind the pack.

He was in the lead, a few feet ahead of the other cyclists, but Meredith thought that even had he been in the middle, she could have picked him out; the polished smoothness of his riding style, the economy and vigor of his practiced movements would have identified him for her.

As much as she enjoyed watching Brandt, now she forced herself to keep her eyes fastened on the road. They were pulling into another town, passing a row of exquisitely restored Victorian cottages painted Easter-egg colors. Spectators stood beside parked cars, waving as the riders passed. Children frolicked on the shoulder.

Then it happened. Out of the corner of her eye Meredith noticed a group of youngsters playing tag beneath a big shady acacia tree in a yard off to the right. The children all appeared to be of grade-school age, except for a tiny girl in a pink romper, who tottered as she tried to run. One of the older boys charged after her, his hands raised in mock menace. The little girl squealed and scampered away, her head craned back in the direction of her pursuer. Her stubby legs carried her off the grass, between parked cars and onto the pavement, directly into the path of Brandt's bicycle.

He had no choice; there was no time to swerve. Locking the brakes, he threw himself sideways and dropped the bike.

Momentum carried him forward several feet, causing him to skid over the unforgiving pavement on his arm and leg. The helmet protected his head, but his gloved hands flew up instinctively to shield his face. One foot became entangled in the chain guard, dragging the bicycle along with him on its crank.

A herd of wheels and cleated shoes whizzed past within inches of his head. People gawked, there were shouts of dismay, and the metallic squeal of hand brakes. Car doors slammed. "My baby!" a woman shrieked.

Brandt lay staring at the sky. A little girl in pink toddled forward and stood over him, solemnly sucking her thumb. Other people joined the child, ringing around him.

"Cripes, guy, are you all—"

"Oh, Lord, will you look—"

"Brandt!"

Meredith dropped to her knees on the asphalt beside him, gasping with fright. He could not see her eyes because of her sunglasses, but her face looked bloodless, as if all life and vitality had been sapped from it. "Oh, Brandt," she whimpered again. "Oh, my poor darling." Her hand hovered over his cheek, vibrating like a moth unable to light.

Her distress tore at him. He wanted to reassure her, take away that look of numb horror. He could tell he was not critically injured, although the burning pain in his side made sweat bead on his mustache. He grimaced and, swallowing with difficulty, he griped, "Damn it, dumped again. This is getting to be a habit with you and me, Merry Forrest."

He was relieved when he saw the corners of her mouth obediently turn up in a smile—not a very convincing one, but a smile nonetheless. "You're right," she replied with forced lightness. "Have you ever considered taking up a less hazardous sport, like skydiving?"

Without waiting for Brandt to respond to her feeble jest, Meredith glanced up at the people huddled about them. She recognized several of the cyclists who had been keeping pace with him, and on the edge of the circle among a cluster of children stood a young couple, their expressions grave and remorseful. The woman was clinging to the toddler in the pink playsuit, her face buried in the child's hair, and the man's arms were wrapped protectively around both of them.

"Please, will someone help me?" Meredith asked. "He's got to be moved. We can't leave him here in the middle of the highway."

Instantly the man with the child stepped forward. "I'm sorry! For a moment there all I could think about was our little girl being okay. If he hadn't reacted so quickly..."

He and two of the racers squatted beside Brandt. "Here, mister, this may hurt a bit—"

Brandt lifted his head. "No," he grated, "don't pick me up. Nothing's broken. I can stand—" He tried to raise himself on his elbow. The jarring pain made him fall back groaning. He held out his hand. "Meredith?"

"Be careful, darling," she said, lacing her fingers through his. "You've left a lot of skin on the road." With the men's help she eased Brandt into an upright position as gently as possible, but she knew they hurt him.

He swayed as he stood and removed his helmet, stiffly rotating his head. The raw flesh on his arm and leg was much less excruciating now that he was no longer lying on it. Regarding himself ruefully, he muttered, "I hope I brought enough Band Aids."

"It's going to take more than first aid," Meredith said. "You need to find a doctor and get that cleaned up."

He scowled. "But there's no time. The race—"

"The race?" she exclaimed, amazement superseding tact. "Are all athletes crazy, or are you just out of your mind with pain?"

"No pain, no gain," he quipped, but despite his humor his face looked gaunt and ashen.

Meredith tempered her tone. "Please, Brandt, listen to me. Forget about adding this year's patch to your collection. You're hurt. You're exhausted. For you the race is over. If you don't believe me, look at yourself."

"I did. I'm a bloody mess. But it doesn't hurt as much now."

Meredith swore succinctly. "If you don't care about your body, look at your bike."

For the first time Brandt allowed himself to glance at the wreckage of his racer. The titanium-alloy frame was twisted out of shape, and one pedal was missing completely; the chain was knotted around the broken derailleur. "Oh, hell," he said inadequately, suddenly feeling very tired.

Meredith noticed the parents of the toddler who'd run out in the road exchange significant looks. His eyes darting to the remains of the obviously expensive bicycle, the young father suggested doubtfully, "I suppose we can pay for the damage? After all, it was our little girl—"

"Forget it," Brandt said in a clipped voice.

Meredith cut in. "If you really want to help, what you can do is direct us to the nearest doctor. Someone needs to tend to those scrapes."

"There's a clinic not half a mile from here. If you want to follow in your car, I could lead you there."

"Thanks." She turned to the other cyclists who hovered nearby, restless and obviously impatient to return to the race. "And thank you, too, for all your help. We really appreciate your stopping, but everything's under control now, if you want to go on." The men grinned their relief and sped away.

While the toddler's father assisted Brandt to the Volvo, Meredith turned to pick up the shattered ten-speed. The bike was a write-off, but perhaps there was some small part of the equipment that could be salvaged. As she stooped, the child's mother, who so far had said nothing, clinging to her daughter in anxious silence, stepped forward.

"Please," she ventured softly, her voice still husky with the fright she had suffered. "I just wanted to tell you how very sorry I am the man got hurt. I happened to look through the kitchen window just as it happened. My God, if he hadn't reacted as quickly as he did, there's no telling what would have happened to Chrissy! It was all my fault, I was busy baking and I thought she was safe playing with the neighbor's kids. But I should have kept better watch on her."

"Don't worry about it," Meredith soothed. "Accidents happen. Kids just get away sometimes."

The woman hugged little Chrissy adoringly. "Yes, they can be a handful, even this sweetie. Do you and your husband have children?"

Meredith shook her head, not bothering to correct the woman's wrong impression. She rather enjoyed being mistaken for Brandt's wife; the idea had a certain appeal. It occurred to her that until that moment she had thought of him only in terms of being her lover. She realized wistfully that she would like very much for him to be her husband, father of her children, someone with whom she could build a stable, satisfying life outside the narrow limits she'd set for herself. She wondered ironically just how long she'd been in love with him without knowing—

"I'm sorry!" Meredith exclaimed, belatedly aware that the woman had been introducing herself. "I didn't catch your name."

"Sally Nash," the woman repeated patiently. "I was just saying that after you've finished at the clinic, if you would like to come back here so that your husband can rest, you're more than welcome."

"That's very kind of you, but we wouldn't want to put you out."

"You wouldn't be putting us out. Taking care of guests is our job." She pointed proudly to a small sign in the center of the yard, its cheery paint still fresh—Nashes' Acacia Lodge. "Jim and I haven't been in the bed-and-breakfast business very long, but I promise you there's not another inn in the valley that could make you any more comfortable." She paused. "It's the least we can do. I don't know how far you two have to go to get home, but I can tell he's not going to feel like doing much traveling right away. We'd be happy to have you, and you're free to stay as long as you like."

Meredith thought about the two-hour drive back to Sacramento. Sally was right; even if the scrapes and bruises he had sustained proved not to be as serious as they looked, Brandt was in no condition to endure that journey. Perhaps in the morning, after he'd had some sleep....

Smiling her gratitude, she said sincerely, "Thank you. We'll be delighted to take you up on that offer."

The doctor in the clinic reinforced Meredith's decision. While Brandt, prone on an examination table, drowsed with his face buried in the crook of his unscathed arm, the physician picked highway grit out of his leg with a pair of tweezers. Meredith sat tensely on an uncomfortable wooden chair, her eyes round with apprehension. Soothingly the doctor said, "I'm glad you've made plans for the night. If you hadn't, I might have had to suggest you admit Mr. Dahlberg to a hospital."

Meredith gasped with dismay. Once his injuries had been cleaned, they appeared far less alarming than she'd thought they were. Now her fears, which had begun to ease slightly, revived. "Good Lord, is it as bad as that?"

"No, but it could have been," the doctor replied grimly. "His body was already in a state of extreme stress from the race, joints weak, muscles exhausted and unresponsive. I see it every May when the racers come through here. By the time they reach this point, the only thing still keeping them going is their minds. Idiots! People ought to have the sense to realize that when the body tells them it's had enough, they should listen."

Meredith gazed resignedly at Brandt's recumbent figure. "He claims it's fun."

"Jocks! Let me tell you—"

Lifting his head, Brandt mumbled blearily, "There's no need for you two to talk about me as if I'm not here. I'm awake. That was only a local anesthetic I had."

"What I should have used was a club, if that's what it takes to knock a little sense into you!" the other man said impatiently. "Apart from the matter of it being sheer luck that you were able to avoid running down that little girl, if you'd fallen differently you could have done serious damage to yourself, irreparable damage." He appraised Brandt's rangy physique with professional disinterest. "You have a fine body here, Dahlberg. Somehow I don't think your lady would appreciate your messing it up, even if you don't care about it."

Brandt was still chuckling tiredly when they left the office. His humor had diminished by the time he collapsed onto the settee in the second-story bed-sitting-room of the Nashes' Victorian cottage. Though his mood was dampened by fatigue, he was still not too tired to appreciate the cozy luxury of the suite.

Fresh flowers in a crystal vase had been placed on the fireplace mantel. A bottle of wine and a basket of homemade cookies, fragrant and warm from the oven, waited on the drop-leaf table. Through the archway he could see Meredith carefully folding back a handcrafted patchwork quilt on the golden oak four-poster. "Jim and Sally's little inn is wonderful," he commented. "Exactly the sort of place I'd hoped you and I could get away to some weekend. I just didn't expect to be . . . out of commission when we did."

"There will be other weekends," Meredith said easily, fluffing a down pillow. A sunbeam angled across the bed, and she stepped to the window to draw the curtains. From her vantage point she could see a neat garden thick with flowers and vegetables behind the house. Sally was moving slowly down a row of staked vines, Chrissy clinging to her skirt, and the two of them were dropping what looked like early Chinese snow peas into a wicker basket.

Beyond the property line a patch of mustard shimmered like living gold in the slanting sunlight; vineyards stretched to the shadowed hills on the western side of the valley. In a distant field one of the hot air balloons Meredith had noticed earlier was tethered. Someone was deflating it, and she watched the bag collapse slowly like a melting rainbow. Yes, she thought poignantly, the Acacia Lodge was a wonderful place to spend a weekend. Perhaps even a honeymoon...

"Meredith," Brandt called.

Closing the curtains, she turned to face him. "I'm sorry. I was distracted by the view. Can I get you something? The bathroom seems to be stocked with toothbrushes, disposable razors and just about everything we'll need, although if there's something else you want, I'm sure one of the Nashes—"

"Meredith," he repeated, stopping her speech, "do you mind the way things turned out?"

She sighed. "I mind like hell that you got hurt, if that's what you mean. I mind that you weren't able to finish your race, which is obviously very important to you."

"Do you mind that right now I'm feeling too sore and worn out to make love to you?"

At the blunt question, Meredith's face reddened, and Brandt realized suddenly that despite their already being lovers, she was still not altogether at ease with him. He found something endearing about her restraint. "Meredith?" he pressed.

She lifted her chin. Tossing back her tumbled hair, she said frankly, "Of course I mind, Brandt. I want you so much I ache. But I can wait."

Brandt gazed hungrily at her, at her slender body in jeans and a tank top that was stained with road dust and— he shuddered—his blood. She was so beautiful, so . . . tolerant. Her burnished curls hung tangled over her weary face, but she seemed completely unaware of her disarray or of her own fatigue. She was concerned only for him.

Selfishly he had dragged her along with him on this race, and all day she had tended him, catering to his whims without complaint, although most of the time she must have been bored to distraction. He doubted he would have displayed the same forbearance had their positions been reversed; he certainly hadn't when he was a boy floundering in that abortive marriage. With gnawing self-awareness he wondered if he'd grown up very much in the years since then.

Even now when Meredith had every right to expect a very personal, very intimate reward for her patience, his needs still took precedence. Flexing his left arm gingerly, Brandt winced with pain and frustration. The mere sight of her was enough to send desire shafting through him like a javelin, but there was no way he could make love to her tonight. No way he could give her the delight and joy she deserved.

Tomorrow...

8

BRANDT DID NOT KNOW if it was the fresh morning breeze drifting in through the fluttering curtains that woke him, or the enticing warmth of Meredith's body in his arms. She had slept fitted spoonlike against him, her back to his bare chest, her lissome legs wound through his. They were sharing the same pillow, and when her hair touched his face, tickling his nose, he sniffled to suppress a sneeze. She stirred uneasily, and his arms tightened around her, drawing her closer. Cupping her breast in his hand, he could feel her nipple press into the palm.

She wriggled in her sleep, her bottom rubbing with maddening provocation across the front of his briefs. As if he needed to be further aroused. . . .

For a very long time he lay quiet, cocooned within downy quilts scented with lavender, savoring the experience of having Meredith beside him. The night before, the raw scrapes on his left side had pained him more than he was willing to admit. He had been too uncomfortable to appreciate the glide of Meredith's capable hands on him as she eased him out of his bedraggled racing shorts and helped him into the bathroom.

By the time Sally Nash had brought up a dinner tray accompanied by a crisp Chablis from one of the local vintners, Brandt was in bed. He was feeling somewhat better after having sponged away the dirt and sweat of the race, but had been able to eat only a few bites before collapsing, spent, against the silky percale sheets.

"Darling, you must sleep," Meredith had whispered with concern, drawing the covers up over his chest. When she leaned over him to brush her lips across his, he had clutched her hand.

"Don't go away," he said, his voice thin, reedy and querulous.

Meredith frowned. "I'm not going anywhere."

"Please," he said urgently, his tired lips shaping an ingratiating smile. "I-I'll rest better with you here beside me."

She recognized that it was debility making him sound so unlike himself. Brandt was a trained athlete accustomed to being in prime physical condition; his prostration bewildered and frightened him. "It's a little early for me to come to bed yet," she told him, adding roguishly, "but if you like, I suppose I could sing you to sleep."

Something flickered in the depths of his eyes. Shaking his head as if to clear it, he said in more normal tones, "Three choruses of 'Rockabye Your Baby with a Dixie Melody'? I'm sorry. I guess I'm just not used to feeling so rotten."

"I know. I know." She kissed him lightly on the forehead. After that she retired to the little couch in the sitting room where she sipped wine and read magazines, glancing broodingly in Brandt's direction from time to time. His fatigue pressed down on him. He had gazed at her through eyes slitted against the incandescent glow of her hair in the lamplight, until at last his drooping eyelids, leaden as his limbs, shut completely.

Still, he had known when she came to bed. Perhaps it was the click of the wall switch that alerted him. His eyes had flicked open again when she stood beside the four-poster. In the darkness he watched catlike as she moved across the room to the window she'd closed earlier.

When she pulled back the curtains, moonbeams spilled over her slender form. She was still clad in the jeans and shirt she'd been wearing since the night before. He chastised himself for having brought a light sweater and slacks—something to put on after the race—and never thinking to suggest Meredith also bring along a change of clothing. He wondered what she would wear to bed, then caught his breath at the thought of her slipping nude between the sheets.

He must have made a sound, for she turned her head to peer into the shadows of the bed. He lay very still. After a moment she removed her glasses and, blinking hazily, placed them on the nightstand. As long as he did not stir, Brandt knew she would not be able to tell he was awake, and for now, while he was still too sore to move, he wanted to watch her unobserved. He wanted the freedom, the simple luxury of looking at her.

She leaned wearily against the sill as she stared blindly into the night, a cool, earth-tanged breeze fluffing her hair. The silvery light robbed her vivid tresses of their fire even as it outlined the pale purity of her profile. Brandt watched in awe as she tossed back her head and stretched her arms high over her head, arching gracefully so that her breasts jutted, high and tempting. When she straightened again, she pulled her tank top loose from her waistband.

Her movements were quick, lithe as she shrugged out of the shirt and laid it neatly folded on the dresser. Brandt's eyes widened as she reached behind her and unsnapped the fastener on her skimpy lace bra, stripping the straps down over her arms. She dropped the bra on top of her shirt, and he had to bite his lip to keep from groaning aloud.

She reached for her belt buckle. Brandt thought he could no longer remain silent, but instead of stepping out of her jeans, she turned away and picked up something white and shapeless from the chair beside the bed. When she slithered it over her head, he recognized the garment as one of his T-shirts. It was much too large for Meredith, the sleeves hanging far off her shoulders, the hem dangling around her thighs. The well-worn cotton knit clung to her when she moved, outlining her high breasts, the sleek curve of her hips; when she dipped to remove her jeans, the front of the shirt ballooned, and he could see bikini panties, sheer and incredibly alluring. His body stirred with an ache almost worse than the one in his bruised side. Damn all bicycles. . . .

When Meredith straightened again, he saw her face. She was gazing dreamily into the shadows of the bed; her ivory features looked naked and defenseless. She looked very, very shy.

She sighed, steeling herself. Brandt had closed his eyes, amazed at how protective he felt. When her slight weight slipped between the sheets beside him, he had flung his arm across her, as if moving in his sleep. For a moment she'd lain tense and rigid beside him, then she'd relaxed and snuggled into the curve of his body. *Tomorrow*, he promised himself once more.

"MEREDITH."

His voice was an elusive whisper on the morning breeze, beating like a moth against the edges of her dreams. His breath ruffled the fine hair on her nape. "Meredith," he murmured again. She shifted restlessly, reluctant to abandon her delicious sleep. Gradually she became aware of the unfamiliar weight lying across her, the sheltering warmth at her back. She could feel long fingers cupping her breast, a callused thumb gently kneading the nipple through flimsy fabric. Moist lips crept along her shoulder. A dark voice teased her ear. "Darling, it's time to wake up."

Red-gold lashes flew up. She tried to recall where she was. Out of the corner of her eye she could see a snowy pillowcase; through the tangled veil of her curls she could just make out the blurred image of a golden oak dresser a few feet away. Her own dressing table at home was teak, Danish modern.

At the window, chintz curtains wafted on a puff of air sweet with the fragrance of wildflowers and rich loam, blossoming grapes. Then she remembered. "Brandt?" she ventured.

"You were expecting someone else?"

He meant the words as a joke, but she took them at face value. "Of course I wasn't expecting someone else," she said quietly. "I've never slept with a man before."

He stared. "What?"

She looked almost embarrassed. "I've never stayed all night with a man. My love life, such as it is, has consisted of fairly brief encounters." She paused, grimacing wryly. "Even you . . ."

From the ardor of her response to him that first time, he'd assumed she was much more experienced. No wonder she seemed such a curious mixture of passion and reserve. Hugging her fiercely, he declared, "There's not going to be anything brief about this encounter, lady. I love sleeping with you. I love having you lie in my arms."

"So do I," Meredith breathed. "I had no idea how wonderful it would be." She touched his mouth, her fingers trembling with need as they outlined his lips coaxingly.

Brushing the hair from her eyes, he framed her face in his hands and stared at her, his expression grave. "You must know by now it's more than just sex, more than just wanting to make love with you, although Lord knows I hunger so much I'm about to go out of my mind. I love you, Meredith. I don't think I've ever felt this way about anyone before."

"Me, neither." She continued to stroke his mouth until at last he nipped at her fingers, worrying the tips between his teeth.

Distractedly he continued, "All my life I've pretty much had everything given to me—my education, my job; even the girl I married started out doing the chasing. But now for the first time I want to be the one who gives. I want you to have everything you want."

"I don't want anything except you," Meredith countered simply. "If you love me, that's enough. Your lips on mine are enough. Your body on mine . . ."

Brandt pulled her down to him, and her words were swallowed by his mouth closing hotly over hers.

More than enough, she thought dizzily when the T-shirt was cast aside and she could feel the feather-soft tickle of his mustache on her breasts, making her nipples pucker in invitation. She held him cradled against her, stroking his fair hair while he sucked gently, and an animal sound welled deep in her throat when his mouth dipped lower. The faint stubble on his chin dragged teasingly across her soft belly, trailing a wake of fire.

"Oh, Brandt!" She clutched wildly at him to halt that crazy slide.

When Brandt lifted his head, his eyes were loving. "Don't stop me, Meredith. This is for both of us."

"But I don't know—"

"You will, darling. I promise. Before we're through, you'll know it all."

"I KNOCKED EARLIER, but when there was no answer, I took your breakfast back down." Sally handed a laden lunch

tray to Meredith, who was hastily tucking her shirt into
the waistband of her jeans. Sally glanced toward the bedroom, where Brandt's still form was a bronzed statue
against the tumbled white sheets. "I didn't want to disturb
your husband. I figured he probably needed his rest more
than food."

Meredith shifted from one bare foot to the other, trying
not to blush. In the dawn light they had made love until,
sated, they could only fall asleep in each other's arms. As
Meredith drowsed, her head on Brandt's chest, the slow,
steady rhythm of his heartbeat beneath her ear had
blended with the chime of a distant church bell floating on
the morning breeze. She had not wakened again until she
heard her hostess's soft knock at the door. "He was a
bit . . . fidgety . . . earlier," she conceded.

"In that case, I'd just let him keep on sleeping as long as
he wants," Sally offered sagely. "It'll do him good. Jim was
going to mow the backyard, but I'll tell him to wait. And
if Chrissy gets too noisy—"

"Oh, don't do that," Meredith exclaimed. "You mustn't
put yourselves out for us. Brandt's going to have to wake
up before too long, anyway, so we can head back to Sacramento."

The other woman looked concerned. "Are you certain
he'll feel strong enough for that tiring drive? There's no
need for you to leave on our account. As we said yesterday, the two of you are welcome to stay as our guests for
as long as you like."

"That's very kind, but there's really no need. He's feeling much better this morning. Besides, surely you must
have other guests arriving?"

Sally shrugged. "There's no one booked before next
weekend. It's a little early in the season yet."

After her hostess left, Meredith padded into the bedroom with the lunch tray. She found Brandt leaning against the pillows, fully alert. "Oh. I thought you were still asleep."

"I woke the minute you slipped out of my arms." He stretched languidly, his expression content to the point of smugness.

"You look very pleased with yourself," Meredith observed lightly. "You're practically smirking."

His grin widened as he extended his hand to her. "Just happy," he said. She set down the tray and caught his fingers in her own. For timeless moments they clung to each other, with no need for words. Then Brandt glanced approvingly at their lunch. "I'm also starving. For some strange reason I've worked up quite an appetite." His eyes darkened provocatively. "You wear me out, lady."

Meredith shivered at his erotic words, but her tone remained dry. "And the fact that you haven't eaten since riding your bike well over a hundred miles couldn't have anything to do with the fact that you're hungry?"

"Oh, no, of course not." He lifted the napkin that covered the tray. "This looks good. Where do you suppose they found wild asparagus?"

When they finished eating, Brandt sighed, replete. "That was delicious. Mrs. Nash is an excellent cook. I'm going to hate to leave."

"They've invited us to stay over again, if we want."

He shook his head regretfully. "Unfortunately, tomorrow is Monday. Back to the salt mines."

"Do you really think you'll feel strong enough to return to work so soon?" Meredith asked with concern.

"Oh, yes. I told you my bumps and bruises aren't nearly as alarming as they must have looked at first. Besides, the way I feel right now, I'll bet I could run all the way back to Sacramento."

He patted the bed in invitation, and Meredith climbed onto the four-poster beside him, curling on top of the coverlet in the crook of his arm. For the moment there was no element of seduction in his embrace, only warmth and communion.

He hugged her cozily and brushed his mouth across the top of her head. "With the exception of taking that spill, it's been a wonderful weekend. Last night I was in no condition to appreciate my surroundings, but looking around now, I don't think we could have picked a better place to stay if we'd planned it. The Nashes have obviously put a lot of work and money into this inn."

Meredith nodded. "I just hope it pays off for them. From something Sally said, I gather they don't have many guests yet."

"Then we'll have to make a point of coming back again soon," Brandt suggested.

"I'd like that." She nuzzled her face against him. In the crisp hair on his chest she could smell her own scent blended with his musky fragrance. That intimate perfume made her dizzy.

"Maybe we can steer some other business their way; recommend the Acacia Lodge as the perfect haven for overworked executives." He hesitated. "Unless, of course, you'd prefer to keep it a secret, our special place."

Meredith smiled, her lips curving against his skin. "Any place you are is already special, darling," she murmured.

Brandt's voice sounded raspy and bemused. "Really? Then let me show you what's so special about you...." Capturing her chin in his fingertips, he tilted her face upward for his kiss. He could taste wine on her mouth, or perhaps it was her essence, sweet and tantalizing.

They did not speak again until they heard Sally Nash calling her daughter into the house for dinner. The slanting beams of the westering sun cast a ruddy glow across the bed once more.

The sun was only a golden memory by the time Brandt sped the Volvo across the freeway bridge arching over the Sacramento River. Between the dark thrusting high rises of the city's deserted downtown area could be glimpsed the ice-white marble walls of the state capitol building, illuminated in the night by spotlights. Few cars moved. Leaning back in the bucket seat, Meredith yawned.

"Home at last. As much as I hated leaving the Nashes, I'm not going to be worth a damn at work tomorrow if I don't get some sleep."

"Funny words coming from a woman who's spent most of the past twenty-four hours in bed," Brandt stated ironically.

"That's why I need the sleep!" Her humor faltered. "Are you really certain you want me to stay the night at your place?"

"Of course. Don't you?"

"You know I do."

"Then I don't understand what the problem is. We'll run by your apartment long enough to pick up a change of clothes for you to wear to the office, and then—"

Meredith said, "But the office *is* the problem, Brandt. I guess I'm going to feel a little strange showing up for work with you in the morning. Isn't that a trifle . . . blatant?"

"Honey," he chided, "it's hardly going to come as a surprise to anybody that we spent the weekend together. I'm certain everyone at Warcom has known for ages how we feel about each other. Haven't you intercepted any of Lois or Annette's indulgent glances, or heard the buzzing whenever we walk down the corridor?"

Meredith sighed, her sense of privacy affronted. "Oh, hell, I suppose you're right, although I can't say I relish the idea of being the hottest topic on the employee grapevine. But office gossip aside, after all that's happened between the two of us, do you honestly think we're going to be able to continue working together as before?"

"Sure, as long as you remember who's in charge," Brandt tossed back flippantly. "Don't forget you're still on probation, and just because you're sleeping with the boss—"

Glancing sidelong at her, he saw her worried expression, and quickly he tempered his tone. He gave her cold fingers a reassuring squeeze. "Look, sweetheart," he said seriously, "in case it's not as clear to you as it is to everyone else, then you should be aware that these past couple of days have meant more to me than just a weekend fling. In addition to making love, we've made a few commitments. We're a team now—same interests, same goals. If anything, working together should be that much easier." As he lifted her hand and brushed his lips across her knuckles, he added mischievously, "And any overtime we put in ought to be a lot more interesting!"

He guided the Volvo to the curb in front of Meredith's apartment complex. "I'll just be a minute," she said, reaching for the door handle.

Brandt scowled as he surveyed the scene. Shifting images filtering through drapes indicated that some of the tenants in the complex were still up, probably watching television, but except for one or two porch lights still burning, the sulfurous security lamps on the corners of each boxy building provided the only illumination outside. The shrub-lined walkways looked shadowed and ominous. He jerked his keys out of the ignition. "I'll go with you."

Meredith smiled gratefully. "Thanks. Although in all the years I've lived here, I've never had any trouble, I have to admit this place gives me the creeps late at night. It'll feel good having a strong man on my arm for once."

As they strolled along the walk, their steps echoed hollowly between the buildings. Brandt suggested calmly, "You know, darling, it doesn't have to be just for this once."

They reached her dark doorstep, and she turned to peer up at him, trying to read his expression in the feeble light. She was almost afraid to believe he'd said what she thought she'd just heard. The expression in his eyes was inscrutable; beneath the mustache his mouth was a straight line. Laying her hand on his chest, through his thin sweater, she could feel his heart lurch.

She swallowed and began tremulously, "Brandt—"

The porch light flicked on. The door flew open with a crash. Mike burst onto the step. "Meredith Forrester, where the hell have you been all weekend? Why did you miss the recording session?"

9

MEREDITH'S HAND FLEW to her mouth. She had never seen Mike so angry. Guilt constricted her throat. "Oh, no," she choked, "it was this afternoon, wasn't it?"

"What recording session?" Brandt asked blankly.

She sighed. "The band was scheduled to put together a demo tape for any promoters who might be at the jazz festival."

"You didn't tell me you had other plans."

She looked up at Brandt in confusion. Did he really imagine she would remember plans when her only concern had been that he recover from the accident? When the two of them were making love, did he expect her to think of her brother? "I had more important things to worry about." To Mike she offered lamely, "I guess I just forgot."

"Forgot!" Mike's face was a mask of irritation and disgust. "How could you forget something so important? What's the matter with you, Merry? You knew we were expecting you to be there!"

"Would you please keep the noise down?" Brandt muttered tightly. Lights had come on in one of the apartments across the walkway from them; curtains fluttered. "We seem to be attracting attention."

"*We* aren't doing anything," Mike retorted with deliberate rudeness. "This is a private discussion between my sister and me. You have no right to interfere. We don't want you here."

Meredith bridled. "Now wait a minute, Mike! In case you've forgotten, this is my home, too. Brandt is welcome to come in whenever he wants." She glanced at Brandt.

His gaze flicked assessingly over Mike. The other man's posture was tense and vaguely threatening. Mildly Brandt suggested, "Your conversation would be a lot more private if you'd continue it indoors, Forrester."

Mike hesitated momentarily, then stepped back out of the way. Once they were inside the apartment, he shut the door firmly behind them. "All right, no one can hear us now. So tell me what happened this weekend."

"I thought you'd already decided what happened this weekend," Meredith snapped, groping for Brandt's hand. "As a matter of fact, most of the time Brandt was resting, trying to recover from a serious accident he had during the bicycle race."

"He looks in pretty good shape to me," her brother judged skeptically.

Meredith couldn't resist. "Oh, he is, he is." She looked up at Brandt, and the glance they exchanged was charged with sensuality. He raised her palm to his lips. When she opened her hand and curved her fingers along the granite ridge of his jaw, she could feel his tongue flick moistly across her lifeline. She shivered.

At the sight of that embrace, Mike averted his face. "I'm surprised at you, Merry."

Regretfully she tucked her arm through Brandt's and returned her attention to her brother. "My personal life is none of your business."

"It is if it involves the band. We sat there for hours waiting for you to show up."

"You should have gone ahead without me."

"Well, after a while, we did—the other guys insisted—but it wasn't the same without you. After all the plans we made, I get sick just thinking about the time we wasted, the hard-earned money—"

Meredith broke in on his tirade, "Do I have to remind you exactly whose money that was? *You* didn't have anything invested in this recording session!"

Mike paled. "Low blow, sis."

"Yes, it was," Meredith whispered, instantly contrite. After all he'd done for her, she had no right to blame Mike because she was now supporting him. "I'm sorry. I shouldn't have said that."

Her brother's shoulders slumped. "Merry, quite apart from the money, you and I both know those tapes are primarily for our personal benefit. We're the only ones who need to impress agents or promoters. None of the others want a career in music; they wouldn't follow up on an offer if it was handed to them on a plate. They're perfectly content to vegetate here in Sacramento for the rest of their lives. But you and me, we're different. We're a team, and we have plans." The plea in his voice tore at her. "You betrayed me."

Meredith winced, and Brandt muttered, "This is becoming a bit melodramatic, isn't it darling? Why don't you grab your clothes and we'll go back to my place."

"Merry—"

Meredith glanced from one man to the other. Mike's features were strained, his eyes dark with hurt. Brandt's tanned face was strangely ashen; he looked worn out. Now that the exhilaration that had buoyed him during their lovemaking had passed, she suspected he was once again feeling the aftereffects of his accident. The two faces she loved best in the world, she thought poignantly, and at the moment she didn't know which man worried her more.

Trying to be reasonable, she said, "Look, can't this conversation wait till later? It's ridiculous to try to talk when we're all exhausted and overwrought."

"I didn't know there was anything left to talk about," Brandt said gruffly. "I thought you and I made some promises to each other this weekend."

Mike's eyes widened. "Promises? Don't tell me you two are planning on—"

Quickly Meredith interrupted him. "You're jumping the gun, brother dear," she grated under her breath. In a firm voice she continued more loudly, "Would you mind leaving us alone for now? Brandt and I need to talk."

Mike stared at her tensely. "All right. If you insist," he replied, shrugging. A moment later she heard his bedroom door close.

Meredith turned gravely to Brandt. Laying her hand lightly on his chest, she said with wistful emphasis, "Brandt, you'll never know how much our time together has meant. Being with you is the most wonderful thing that's ever happened to me."

"Then what are we arguing about? Why aren't you busy packing your clothes to move in with me?"

Her smile was ironic. "Maybe because you didn't ask me."

He responded instantly. "Meredith, will you come live with me?"

She hesitated, uncertain how to answer. Yes, she wanted to live with him, sleep with him; she thought that someday she'd like to bear his children. *Someday.* Right now, there were too many obligations already demanding her attention. Her voice faltered as she repeated, "Live with you? That's a big decision to make on the spur of the moment."

"It isn't if you love me."

"I do love you, Brandt," she said, sighing. "But I love other people, too—Mike, the guys in the band."

"Your adoring fan club," he muttered.

"Well, we have been together a long time," she pointed out gently. "But there's no reason for you to be jealous. My loving them doesn't mean I love you any less."

Brandt gazed down into Meredith's wide eyes, guarded behind the reflective lenses of her glasses. He was so used to seeing her wearing those glasses that he scarcely noticed them except when they were gone...when she stared up dreamily from her pillow, her hair a corona of flame about her glowing face. He'd never realized glasses could form a barrier between them, shielding her thoughts from him. "I've always heard love involved commitments," he countered.

"It does. That's why I can't just ignore the other people in my life."

"Then you're saying your commitments to them are stronger than your commitment to me?"

His persistence was beginning to irritate her. Why couldn't he see there was nothing wrong with having more than one loyalty? She thought of her brother, so alone, so vulnerable in his determination to reach the goal their parents had failed to attain. She remembered the guys in the band, whom she had dismissed from her mind lately; they had goals, too.

Mike had suggested the demonstration tape was really only for him and Meredith, but he was wrong. Even if the other musicians of the New Helvetia Jazz Society were basically amateurs, they had been looking forward to having a professionally engineered recording of their mu-

sic, a treasure to share with family and friends. She was
their friend, or at least she was supposed to be. They'd
been working together for a long time, and she owed them
an apology for treating them in such a cavalier manner.

She declared flatly, "Brandt, I will not let you goad me
into making a choice between you and my friends."

"I'm not trying to goad you into anything," he insisted.
"I just don't know what to think anymore, not about us,
not even about your job. Once you told me you'd never
let anyone stop you from getting what you want out of life.
I thought you were talking about working with me at
Warcom. But now I wonder if you were saying that only
because you wanted a high-paying job to tide you over
while you work with your band. Are you going to leave
the company—and me—the minute your show business
career takes off?"

Meredith stiffened. "Listen to me, Brandt Dahlberg. I
have told you I love you. I have told you that my singing
has no bearing on the fact that I want a career in applied
mathematics, preferably at Warcom. And if my word isn't
good enough for you, then there's something deeply, basically wrong with our relationship, something that
sleeping together is not going to remedy." She shook her
head in exasperation. "If you hounded Cynthia like this,
it's no wonder she left—" She broke off, but too late.

At the unforgivable words, Brandt's eyes glinted like
Arctic ice. "I think you're right, Meredith," he said curtly,
his voice clipped and low. "It's obvious we've both made
a serious mistake. In that case, I guess I'd better be going."
His posture rigid, he turned on his heel and stalked away

Meredith closed the front door quietly and walked down
the hallway to her room. When she saw the ragged teddy
bear sitting on her pillow, she burst into tears.

She cried until the pillow sham beneath her face was sodden with a mixture of salty tears and melted mascara. By the time the outburst subsided into throaty whimpers, her eyes burned and her headache raged worse than ever, a band of pain constricting her skull like a metal strap. Her jaw hurt, and she realized she'd been holding it clamped shut to keep from blubbering aloud. She felt drained. Worse, she felt like a fool. She hadn't cried since her parents died.

Oh, damn and blast him, anyway. Weary and disgruntled, she shoved the teddy bear out of sight under the dust ruffle of her single bed. And damn her brother. Why did both of them suddenly have to become so possessive?

Her depressing train of thought was interrupted by a tentative knock on the bedroom door. "Merry?" Mike called hesitantly through the thickness of the wood. "May I talk to you, please?"

She sighed and sat up. "Come on in."

He pushed open the door gingerly. Poking his dark head into the room, he held out a steaming mug. "I heard your friend leave. I thought you might want some coffee." After putting on her glasses, she accepted the proffered cup in silence and motioned for him to take her vanity stool. Watching her shuttered expression as she drank, Mike ventured hopefully, "Truce?"

"Truce?" Meredith repeated quizzically. "How about a surrender? My terms. Michael David Forrester solemnly swears never ever to intrude into his sister's private life again. So help him God."

"Merry, I can't promise not to worry about you."

"There's no need to worry. I've told you I'm an adult, and I can take care of myself. But whether you believe that or not, I won't have you butting in the way you did tonight."

"Now, wait just a minute. You're talking as if you're the only injured party. I have a few gripes of my own about what happened today, you know. Have you forgotten the way you left me and the others in the lurch over the recording session? Talk about waste! Not just money, but time, people. The studio was rented, the sound engineer hired, everyone set up and ready to go—and we couldn't do anything, because you weren't there."

"I thought you said you went ahead and recorded the instrumentals."

"We did. But without you it just wasn't the same. We need you. Without your vocals the New Helvetia Jazz Society is just another local band, suitable for entertaining at bar mitzvahs and company picnics."

Frowning into her coffee cup, Meredith said, "That's not true. You, Don, the other guys, you're all good musicians."

"But when you're with us, we're better than good. Why do you think Jack Barnes always insists you be there when he hires us for a gig at Sonora Sue's? You inspire us, Merry. You're the heart of the band."

She felt flattered, flustered, bewildered. "Why, what a lovely thing to say. I-I had no idea."

His smile was indulgent. "Good grief, sis, no wonder you wear glasses. Everyone else has seen it all along. Mom and Dad knew it the moment you were born. There's something about you that radiates... charisma, I guess you'd call it. Why do you think the folks shoved me aside and made you the centerpiece of the act while you were still only a baby? Why do you think they kept pushing you when you said you wanted out? They knew the only way they'd ever make it to the top would be riding on your coattails, because *you* are the one Forrester with real talent, with star quality."

This time when he chuckled, there was an unpleasant edge to his laugh. "And the hell of it is, you don't even want it!"

Meredith stared at her brother as if he was a stranger. Across the room from her he perched on the teak stool in front of her dressing table, his elbows on his knees, his shoulders slumped. Beneath a dangling lock of hair his coldly handsome face was pinched and sallow, his eyes narrowed, focused intently on some point beneath the floorboards. He looked almost . . . bitter.

An astonishing and distasteful thought formed in Meredith's mind. Swallowing painfully, she asked, "Mike, are you jealous of my talent?"

The question hung ticking between them, but then he shrugged, and the moment was defused. "I used to be," he admitted frankly. "When we were kids, I resented the fact that your performing skills were the only thing that seemed to matter to our parents. All I wanted was to please Mom and Dad, but no matter how hard I practiced, they never let me solo.

"When I was about fifteen, I showed Dad an arrangement I'd been working on secretly for weeks, a ragtime medley that just happened to include a long cornet obbligato I could handle. He glanced over the chart, said 'There's no part for Merry,' and tossed it aside."

Meredith flinched. "You must have hated me."

"Of course I didn't hate you," Mike contradicted, shaking his head. "You were all of about ten at the time. Nobody hates his baby sister." He sighed. "But I did decide that as soon as I reached eighteen and scraped together a little money, I was going to take off on my own. Los Angeles, Las Vegas, maybe even New Orleans. Where I went didn't matter as long as there were jobs for musicians and I was judged on my talent. Instead . . ." His voice faded.

Meredith finished for him. "Instead, when you turned eighteen, the folks died and you stayed in Sacramento to raise me. Maybe it would have been better if you'd let me go to a foster home."

"I could never do that," Mike declared flatly. "You were my sister, all I had in the world. I cared about you."

"And I care about you, too, big brother."

Jumping to his feet, he began to stalk the room. "Merry," he began earnestly, "please believe me when I tell you I have never regretted the sacrifices I made for you. We're family; nothing else matters. But the fact remains that at a critical time in my life I abandoned my own and our parents' ambitions because you needed me."

"I know. I'll always be in your debt."

Mike halted his agitated pacing and stood in the center of the room, peering down at her. "Exactly. And now I'm calling in that debt. I need you. When I was eighteen, I wanted to make it on my own, but now I'm too old to have scruples about using you to get my career going. I want you to do whatever you have to to help me. You know as well as I do, as well as our folks did, that you could break into the big time if only you'd push a little. I want you to push."

"Even if I don't want to? C'mon, Mike, it doesn't work that way. The notion of someone becoming a star in spite of herself sounds very dramatic on soap operas, but this is reality. Talent and luck aren't enough. Nobody makes it to the top without intense drive, a ruthless obsession with success. I don't have it. I'm a very private person. I'd hate being famous."

Mike said impatiently, "I'm certain you'd enjoy the limelight a lot more than you're willing to admit, Merry. Despite your claim that you enjoy your high-tech job, it's music that's in your blood. You know you love to sing."

"Yes, but not as a way of life. I—"

He squelched her objections. "I'm not sure I much care how you feel about singing as long as sooner or later some promoter notices me clinging to your coattails. At my age I'm not too proud to play second fiddle. I want that career I gave up for you—sooner or later. But I'd prefer it was sooner."

Licking her lips, Meredith asked, "After all this time, why the sudden rush?"

"Because I'm not a kid anymore," Mike said deliberately. "Because I'm twenty-nine years old, and my sister supports me. Because I have absolutely nothing to offer the woman I want to marry."

Meredith's eyes widened in joyous revelation as she stared at her brother. "Oh, Mike," she breathed. "You've found someone at last. I used to worry it was because of me that . . . I'm so happy for you. Falling in love is wonderful."

"That's how the old song goes, anyway," he conceded, grinning sheepishly. After a moment his smile dimmed. "Sometimes I'm not so sure."

"Why not?" she demanded indignantly, her sisterly hackles rising at the thought of anyone daring to reject her beloved brother. "Doesn't she love you?"

Mike sighed. "She says she feels the same way I do, but how would she know? She's just a child."

"Child?" Meredith's face mirrored her confusion as she tried to analyze that odd word. After a moment she recalled images of a petite brunette with infatuated eyes; a sheet of music manuscript for a romantic melody dedicated to C. She said, "It's that Cheryl, isn't it? The teenager who lied to you about her age. I didn't know you were still seeing her."

"I guess I was embarrassed to tell you," Mike admitted, "especially after the fuss I made when I found out how young she was. But she kept coming back. Not to bars—I really yelled at her for using fake identification to get into Sonora Sue's—but whenever the band had a gig in a pizza parlor or someplace where there were no age restrictions, she was always there, sitting in the front row.

"At first I tried to ignore her; I figured getting involved with someone that young would just be asking for trouble. But she's so pretty, and so persistent, and eventually I started talking to her during the breaks."

"What do you and an eighteen-year-old have to talk about?"

"Oh, lots of things—she's very bright, very mature for her age—but mostly we talked about music. It turns out she's majoring in piccolo at Sac State. She was telling the truth about being in college, after all, except she's a freshman not a senior. Her whole family are jazz buffs. Her parents have been involved with the Dixieland Jubilee almost from the beginning."

"Sounds like your kind of people," Meredith noted. "You should have no trouble winning their approval."

"I haven't asked for their approval. I haven't asked Cheryl to marry me. I don't know if I ever will."

"But I thought you told me—"

"Be realistic, Merry," Mike said thickly. "An unemployed musician eleven years older than the girl is not exactly the kind of suitor most fathers will welcome with open arms. For that matter, it's not the kind of husband I want to be."

"You'd be a great husband—or does being older bother you that much?"

"No. Considering all the other things Cheryl and I have in common, I don't think I'd mind the age difference much at all, if only I had something else to offer her. That's why I need you to help me become established. A wife needs a home, security. . . ."

Driven by her brother's obvious pain, Meredith pointed out, "Our parents never had a home or security."

Mike's mouth quirked. "Would you of all people ask someone you love to live the kind of life Mom and Dad did?"

"No," Meredith responded bluntly. "But I also wouldn't ask someone I love to jeopardize his own relationships in order to help me work out mine."

For a long while brother and sister regarded each other in silence. There didn't seem to be anything to say.

At last Meredith picked up her coffee mug from the nightstand. The dregs were cold and scummy. Grimacing at the unappetizing sight, she muttered, "I must rinse this out," but before she could stand, Mike removed the cup from her fingers.

"I'll take care of it," he said. "You'd better try to get some sleep. You've got to go to work in the morning."

Work! Meredith glanced at the alarm clock on her dresser, astonished by the time. So little of the night remained that she doubted it was worthwhile even going to bed. Maybe she should just bathe and change her clothes. She'd been wearing the same outfit for almost forty-eight hours. She felt unbearably grungy.

On the other hand, she supposed a little rest was better than none at all. Sighing windily, she reached for her pillow to fluff it. There was a brown smudge of makeup on the sham, evidence of the emotion that had racked her earlier, after Brandt left. She stared at it, transfixed, wondering how she was going to face him after the weekend they'd just spent, ecstasy followed by disillusion and acrimony.

From the doorway she heard Mike say soberly, "Merry, I know what I'm asking of you; I know you'd rather be with your new man than with your brother. It's only natural. But I'm family, and you owe me for the way I put off my career when you needed me. Now I need you. Please don't fail me."

He closed the door quietly behind him. Meredith turned back the coverlet on her bed. Unzipping the sham, she removed the pillow from its case and with great precision arranged it squarely on the exposed sheets. She took off her glasses and folded them carefully on the nightstand. Her headache was worse than ever; the swaying movements of her body as she slithered out of her sweat-stained tank top made her temples throb. Despite her bone-numbing weariness, she knew she was never going to get to sleep.

10

"HEY, WAIT FOR US!" Lois called as she and Annette scurried out of the Warcom parking lot to catch up with Meredith at the side entrance. Meredith halted in front of the glass doors and waited patiently for her friends, absently murmuring greetings to other employees who streamed past her into the building. A lopsided smile was pasted insecurely on her lips; she hoped it stayed in place.

But when the other women joined her, Annette peered into her face and asked worriedly, "Are you all right? You look like hell."

"Gee, thanks. You're really great for my ego," Meredith responded in a bantering tone.

"You do look tired," Lois judged kindly. "Are you sure you're not coming down with something? I hear there's some new flu going around. Or maybe it was just a busy weekend?"

Meredith could feel her cheeks grow warm as she stammered, "Well, I—that is—"

Annette declared, "I'll bet you've been rehearsing for the jazz festival, right? I think it's so exciting that you're going to sing in it! I've attended several times in the past, but this will be the first year I've ever actually known one of the—"

A deep voice cut in, "I beg your pardon, ladies, I'd like to get to the door."

Nudging the others back, Meredith muttered absently, "I'm sorry. We didn't mean to block the way." Her voice

faded when she looked over her shoulder to see Brandt
looming just behind them, his cycling helmet dangling
from one gloved hand. He was dressed in a sleeveless jersey and shorts, and the snowy gauze bandages on his arm
and thigh glared against his tan. Sweat dewed his forehead. On his throat was a purplish bloom that Meredith
knew had been caused not by the accident but by her own
teeth. Swallowing hard, she whispered, "Oh. Hello."

He nodded curtly. "Meredith."

She recoiled as if he'd slapped her. After the harsh
charges exchanged the evening before, she had expected
their meeting this morning to be difficult, cautious while
they tiptoed gingerly around the unexploded words that
lay strewn between them. She had not expected him to
treat her like a stranger.

Brandt looked past her to the other two women. "Good
morning, Lois, Annette. If you'll excuse me—" Gray lines
of strain bracketed his mouth as he tried to stride past
them. His gait was stiff, labored.

Lois exclaimed in dismay, "Brandt, you're limping! Are
you hurt?"

"I . . . had a slight accident this weekend. I'll be all right.
Thank you for your concern." Carrying himself rigidly, he
stalked away toward the elevator.

Turning to the other women, Lois declared, "It sure
looks to me as if it was more than a 'slight' accident! I know
Brandt must take a spill now and then on that bike of his,
but I've never seen him so banged up. What do you suppose happened?"

Before Meredith could speak, Annette responded, "If I
remember correctly, this past weekend was that big race
he rides in every year, the one my son canceled out on.
Brandt must have found someone else to drive along with

him. I'm glad. I know the race means a lot to him, even if
he does always look washed out for days afterward."

"Well, that's to be expected, after two hundred miles,"
Lois agreed. "I hope it's just fatigue and a few scratches;
I'd hate to think he'd really gotten hurt." She turned to
Meredith. "Why don't you find out what happened and
then tell us all about it at lunch?"

The thought of facing her friends' innocent questions
made Meredith feel faint. Quickly she improvised, "Well,
I-I was thinking about skipping lunch."

"For heaven's sake, Meredith, I hope you're not diet-
ing!" Annette reproved. "You certainly don't need it."

Lois said, "You have to come to lunch! I have some news
of my own."

"Oh, all right," Meredith acquiesced, shrugging weakly.
She'd field their questions somehow. In the meantime she
was relieved that nobody seemed to suspect the truth of
her relationship with Brandt. She wasn't sure she'd be able
to continue working at Warcom if everyone knew what
had happened between them.

She wasn't sure how long she'd be able to continue
working there, anyway, she admitted with a groan as she
entered her office and heard the shower running in
Brandt's dressing room.

Only a few feet away, the man she loved was standing
naked in that stark tile stall, water drenching his pale hair,
dripping from his mustache into the mouth she'd kissed,
sluicing over the rangy, muscular body she had previ-
ously bathed with her tongue. . . . The memory made her
quiver.

Meredith sat down at her desk and pulled out a report
she'd been reviewing Friday at quitting time. The long
columns of numbers blurred and danced before her eyes.
Laying down her pencil, she removed her glasses and me-

thodically polished the lenses with a tissue. She settled the frames precisely onto the bridge of her nose again, and returned her attention to her work. If she and Brandt didn't resolve their situation soon, she admitted, the frustration of seeing him daily without being able to touch him was going to push her to the breaking point.

He did not speak to her all morning. Meredith's desk was stacked with files and documents demanding her attention, and by accident or design, the one time she ventured into the inner office with a question about some incomplete sales figures, Brandt was talking on the telephone. As he leaned back in his swivel chair, his long gabardine-clad legs crossed in front of him, he stared blindly out the picture window, and he motioned distractedly for Meredith to leave the papers with him. Later, while she stepped across the hallway to the women's lounge, the report reappeared on her desk, Brandt's terse comments scrawled in the margin.

"Well, perhaps poor Brandt's just not feeling good," Lois suggested at lunchtime in the cafeteria, after Meredith gave her and Annette a carefully edited description of the friction between her and her boss. The three women were seated together in the middle of a long table crowded with clerical workers and technicians from the manufacturing wing, most of whom eavesdropped avidly on any gossip that filtered down from the executive suites on the fifth floor. Lois said, "Even if we don't know exactly what happened to him this weekend, it's obvious the guy's had some kind of accident. He moves as if he's sore."

Annette noted dryly, "According to my staff, Brandt Dahlberg always acts sore if things don't go to suit him! You work with him every day, Meredith—what do you think?" Meredith remained silent, her expression blank. When she did not speak, Annette sighed and continued,

"You're probably right, Lois. Brandt doesn't seem to be feeling well. We're just so used to him being the invincible athlete that it's hard to imagine him in less than top physical condition. But when I passed him in the corridor on the way down here, he looked . . . I don't know, tired or depressed or something. Maybe he ought to go home and rest."

"He can't go home," Lois countered, her affable smile thinning. "When I got to my office, I discovered Walter's not here today either. One of the two of them has to be on hand to take charge of things in case of emergencies."

"Where's Mr. Warren?" inquired a girl dressed in the technicians' unofficial uniform of jeans and T-shirt. "He hasn't come down with the flu, has he?"

Lois stared at the luncheon plate before her. Jabbing her fork into a tremulous gelatin salad, she muttered in clipped tones, "As far as I know, Mr. Warren enjoys perfect health. He left a note indicating he'd be in the Lake Tahoe area for a day or two. Family business, I suppose."

Unwillingly Meredith's eyes met Annette's above their friend's lowered head. Lake Tahoe was the location of the sanitarium where Walter's wife resided.

After a moment Lois straightened her shoulders and pushed away her meal, uneaten. She declared, "Speaking of people taking a rest, I just found out that I am about to depart on a long-overdue vacation next Saturday. To Mexico."

"Wow! How'd you manage that, win a quiz show?" someone farther along the table asked.

"Oh, no, nothing so exciting," Lois explained breezily. "Actually, although it's a wonderful opportunity for me, in a way it's rather sad. Months ago my sister and her husband booked passage on one of those 'love boat' cruises to Mazatlan. Then day before yesterday, after waiting eagerly all this time, my sister's boy and his father were shooting baskets in their driveway, and my brother-in-law slipped on an oil spot and somehow managed to break his tibia in three places. Poor guy's going to be laid up for weeks. It's too late to cancel the trip without losing all the deposits they paid, so my sister called and asked me to go with her, instead."

"Gee, Lois, it's too bad about your brother-in-law," someone commiserated, "but are you sure you didn't pour that oil on the driveway yourself?"

In the midst of the good-natured teasing that followed, Meredith muttered under her breath, "What's Walter going to say about you taking off on such short notice?"

Lois shrugged, her expression oddly defiant. "Considering all the years I've arranged my time off to suit *his* convenience—when I haven't canceled my plans altogether—Walter Warren is not in much of a position to say anything. In any case, he'll probably just laugh and ask me to bring him back some genuine Mexican jumping beans for his toy collection."

At the bitter undertone in the secretary's usually sweet voice, Meredith and Annette exchanged glances again. Then Annette tactfully redirected the conversation by declaring briskly, "Well, Lois, we all hope you have a great time on your trip. You certainly deserve it. But just make sure you come home in time for the Dixieland Jubilee. You don't want to miss the chance to hear Warcom's very own star perform."

Talk around the lunch table shifted to the topic of the festival. Even those women who knew no more about traditional jazz than they did about Elizabethan madrigals seemed genuinely interested in Meredith's role in the upcoming event. Their support and encouragement warmed her. As they chattered and joked, she began to realize how

very constricted her life had been to date, lived almost ex-
clusively in the company of men whose one abiding passion was their music. Only rarely did she enjoy the
camaraderie of other women. Apart from the fact that she
valued her job at Warcom, she would not, could not, give
up the friendship of the people she worked with—not to
help her brother, not even to get away from Brandt.

Ironically, just as she was totting up the reasons why she
intended to stay with the firm, someone chuckled. "Maybe
we ought to get Meredith's autograph now while we have
the chance. Once she leaves Sacramento to become rich
and famous—"

"Oh, no, don't talk about her leaving yet!" groaned another of Annette's subordinates dramatically. "If she does,
one of us will have to fill in for her until Mr. Dahlberg hires
a replacement, and we still haven't recovered from the last
time his assistant split! The data-entry people were
threatening to take a strike vote if we ever got left to his
not-so-tender mercies again."

The young technician who'd asked about Walter earlier frowned. "I don't understand why you people on the
fifth floor think Mr. Dahlberg is such a tyrant to work for.
When he comes down to the clean-rooms to check things
out, he's always very polite. Everyone likes him. In fact,"
she added ingenuously, "considering what a hunk he is,
most of us are half in love with him."

"Don't you people have better things to do than fantas-
ize about your employer?" Annette said repressively.

The girl blushed. "Well, gosh, Mrs. Nakatani," she de-
fended, "Mr. Dahlberg's so gorgeous..." She looked
pleadingly at Meredith. "You work for him. Don't you
think he's a doll? When you see him running around in
those shorts of his, don't you ever try to imagine the kind

of things that might go on on that couch in his private office?"

Everyone grew still, all gazing with silent expectation at Meredith, and she realized that she'd been mistaken. Although nobody knew she and Brandt had gone away together, many of them had obviously sensed the growing attraction between them. Shrugging, she rallied, "Oh, sure. Once an hour I take time off from the computer printouts to moon over Brandt Dahlberg. And if I finish my work early enough, we have an orgy during the coffee break." She was pleased and relieved when everyone laughed, dispelling her anxiety.

Her composure faltered when an elbow nudged her in the side and she glanced up to see Brandt seated two tables away. The hand holding his fork was frozen midway between his plate and his mouth. He was glaring at her.

When she returned to the fifth floor, he was waiting. The instant she slid out the bottom drawer of her desk to put away her handbag, the intercom buzzed and Brandt barked, "Ms Forrester, come into my office at once!"

Her eyes flashed angrily at his tone, but when she stood in the connecting doorway between their offices, her expression was frosty. "You called—sir?"

He stared at her, noting the squareness of her shoulders, her unyielding posture. "Meredith," he declared with a heavy sigh, "you may be planning on leaving Warcom as soon as you get that show-business offer you've been waiting for, but I work here. I have a reputation to maintain. Despite the events of the past weekend, I would appreciate it very much if you would refrain from bragging to the typing pool about your exploits with me!"

Stung, she hurled back fiercely, "Damn you, Brandt Dahlberg, I am not a gossip. And even if I were, after the way you've tried to make me ashamed of what happened between us, I hardly think my exploits, as you so quaintly put it, are something I'd care to brag about." She was glad when she saw him flinch.

Pausing, she inhaled and added, "You might as well know now that no matter how unpleasant you make things for me, I have no intention of quitting Warcom. I like the company, I like my work and, what's more, I'm good at it. Hound me all you want, but I will not leave unless you fire me."

He waved aside her words testily. "Meredith, there's no need to lie about your plans. You made it very clear last night that you are under no obligation to me. All I ask of you is the courtesy of two weeks' notice when you decide to go, so that I won't be stuck the way I was when your predecessor lit out for his ashram in Oregon. I do have schedules to maintain, you know."

Somehow the notion that he believed she would behave so unprofessionally was the last straw. "You bastard," she snapped. "It would serve you right if I did take off!"

The rugged planes of his beautiful, beloved face looked slack, weary and resigned. "Just don't expect severance pay if you do," he muttered. Turning away, he went back to his work.

THE REMAINING WEEKS until the opening of the Dixieland Jubilee were a blur to Meredith. Tense and dizzy, she was more convinced with each passing day that she was approaching a crisis in her life.

At night she rehearsed with her brother's band and added her input to weighty discussions about exactly which numbers the group should play in each of its twelve scheduled appearances during the four-day festival. There would also be informal jam sessions that would go on until dawn. When she wasn't polishing her vocal technique, she listened attentively to the other members and offered enthusiastic encouragement whenever one of them broke into a flashy solo or otherwise stretched beyond his previous limits as a musician. She ran endless errands to the tailor who was outfitting the men and to the haberdasher to pick up the jaunty straw skimmers that completed their roaring-twenties-style costumes. Somewhere she located a pair of Cuban-heeled pumps for herself and found time to let out the bodice of the fringed silk flapper dress. The one thing she balked at was Mike's sudden brainstorm that she should bob her hair.

By day she tried to cope with Brandt's repressive behavior. His bandages had disappeared, the scratches faded, but the painful strain between the two of them remained. Brandt behaved with distant civility, as if those two magic days in the Napa Valley had never happened, as if they were strangers united solely by their work.

His disconcerting conduct reminded her of how he had acted that first dreary week she worked for him. But now each day passed without any sign of a thaw in his attitude. The only thing that gave her the fortitude to continue with her work was a nagging suspicion—or maybe it was wishful thinking—that he was as depressed as she was.

"I GOTTA RIGHT to sing the blues." Louis Armstrong's sawtoothed voice rumbled hollowly through the empty apartment. Meredith was taking advantage of the first night in ages when the group was not rehearsing. The musicians had agreed that everyone should take a couple of nights off to prevent burnout and to garner energy for the exhausting schedule they faced over the Memorial Day weekend. Mike was off somewhere with Cheryl, and

Meredith lounged with a glass of white wine and sewed rhinestones on a velvet headband that was the same bright blue as the stripes on the men's blazers.

The long boxes containing the men's jackets and white pants were stacked beside her on the couch; she had picked them up from the tailor late that afternoon. Once the guys dropped by the apartment to get their costumes, everything would be ready. There was nothing left to do but wait for the parade that opened the festival.

As Meredith attached beads to the ribbon with tiny meticulous stitches, she tried to hum along with the record. In the stillness of the apartment the music seemed morosely appropriate, even if it was in the wrong key for her to sing. Sipping her chablis, she frowned and recalled that somewhere among her numerous records was a later rendition of the same song by Billie Holiday, in a range Meredith could handle. Not that she ever expected to match the other woman's artistry, of course, despite her brother's definitely biased opinion of her talents, but she hadn't played the record in a long time. It would be nice to listen to it again—assuming, of course, that she could locate it among the albums and 78-rpm singles in bulky fiberboard jackets that lay scattered all around the stereo.

Laying aside her sewing, she set her wineglass on the coffee table beside a snapshot she'd received in the mail earlier that day, an instant print of Lois and some unidentified male tourist perched on burros on a beach in Mexico. Lois looked relaxed and glowing, or perhaps it was just the tan she'd acquired. In any case, she appeared to be enjoying her vacation.

Meredith knelt on the carpet in front of the phonograph and began to thumb through the record collection. She tried not to remember the evening Brandt had done exactly the same thing.

The records were much as they'd left them that night—
jumbled haphazardly, swing mixed with Dixieland, Scott
Joplin lying alongside Thelonious Monk. When she finally had some free time, Meredith decided, she'd restore
order and update her lists of albums. The work had been
started years before; on many of the covers were glued
yellowing labels covered with neat rows of faded femi-
nine handwriting—her mother's handwriting.

Meredith's parents might have been the most disorgan-
ized people in the world, but they had meticulously cat-
aloged their jazz collection by artist and composer, with
additional notes on structure and style. They probably
could have cited the dates of every record they owned.
Meredith was not so sure they would have remembered
her birthday so easily.

The telephone rang. Startled, Meredith jumped up and
dashed to the kitchen. Breathlessly she said hello.

"Merry Forrest?" Brandt had meant to sound teasing,
but his voice came out oddly gruff.

Her voice was full of genuine delight. "Brandt? I-I was
just thinking about you."

"Trying to figure out how you're going to scrape up the
courage to face yet another day with the Fiend of the Fifth
Floor?" he asked dryly.

"What?"

"Isn't that what the women in clerical are calling me
lately? I hear they're making book on how much longer
you'll be able to stand working for me." He hoped she realized his acid mockery was directed at himself; her
cheerful sarcasm reassured him.

"If the girls in clerical knew me better, they'd realize I'm
too stubborn to let myself be hounded out of a job I like
just because my boss is an arrogant, ill-tempered crank."

He coughed. "Be patient with me, Meredith. Even we arrogant, ill-tempered cranks have occasional good days."

"I know," Meredith said bleakly. "I remember them well."

For a long moment he was silent, trying to frame the words he'd planned to say, his diffident apology. He knew he was a jerk for being jealous of Meredith's brother and her friends and all the other people who were drawn to her vibrancy the same way he was; he knew he had no right to expect her to give up their adulation for that of one grumpy, boring engineer. But if she truly meant what she said about loving him, and could be patient with his insecurities . . . Exhaling loudly, he blurted, "Meredith, are you happy with the way things are between us?"

"Darling, do you really have to ask?"

Her casual endearment shivered through him. "No, of course not," he conceded. "It's a stupid question. I guess I'm feeling mixed up. But that's the way it seems to be with you and me. We get along beautifully when it's only the two of us, then other people interfere and suddenly everything becomes very confused. If we could find someplace quiet and private where we could talk—"

"Just . . . talk?"

There was a provocative edge to her voice that raised goose bumps on Brandt's arms; if he didn't touch her soon, he was going to explode. "Well, we could talk for a little while, anyway," he said throatily.

"Brandt," Meredith suggested, "I'm alone here at home right now. There are jazz records on the stereo and about half a gallon of so-so California chablis, although I suppose if you're prejudiced against jug wine, you could stop somewhere and get something better."

"To hell with the wine." His words were almost a groan.

"Then I'll expect—" Her words were drowned out by a sudden racket that arose in the background, the noise and laughter of a large group of people.

"What did you say?" Brandt asked.

Meredith almost had to shout back, "I'm sorry. It sounds as if one of the other tenants is throwing a party. There are a whole bunch of people coming up the sidewalk. I said—"

The front door of Meredith's apartment banged open, the sound of the crash jarring even over telephone wires. Brandt heard Mike Forrester bellow, "Hey, sis, get up, nap time's over!" The opening measures of reveille blared shrilly from his horn.

A confused clatter indicated Meredith had almost dropped the telephone. "Good grief," she exclaimed, "Mike and Cheryl have brought the entire band back with them, and half their wives! Thank heavens they also appear to have picked up some chips and beer! And there's Jack Barnes, and another couple I don't recognize."

Brandt felt his spirits sink. Her adoring crowd. He'd never be able to compete with them. He heard some man yell, "Surprise, Merry, love, surprise! Mike and his lady bumped into the rest of us coming out of Sonora Sue's, and when he told us our outfits were ready and also said you needed something to liven you up, we all decided to retire here to pick up the blazers and do some serious celebrating! After all, in a couple of days we're going to be stars!"

"Oh, Brandt," Meredith apologized weakly.

In bracing tones he observed, "Must be quite a crowd."

"It is . . . and it's liable to get even bigger. Knowing this bunch, the festivities could very well go on until dawn, and neighbors will probably drop by to complain about the noise and then stay to join the fun." She sighed. "I know it's not what we had in mind, but why don't you come on over anyway?"

The last thing Brandt wanted was to have to share Meredith with a roomful of rowdy, drunken musicians. With impeccable courtesy he said, "Thank you, but no. I'm afraid it doesn't really sound like my kind of party."

She suggested hopefully, "I could probably slip away after a while and come to your place?"

Oh, hell, what was the use? "No, Meredith, don't do that. I wouldn't dream of tearing you away from your friends. I'll see you at work. Goodbye, darling." His fingers left clammy handprints on the receiver as he quietly hung up the telephone.

11

"MERRY, PLEASE SIT STILL!" Mike begged. "I promise you're not going to fall off."

"I don't believe you," Meredith retorted shakily from her insecure perch on the roof of the panel truck. The van shivered, its motor idling in preparation for the start of the parade. Festoons of gay helium-filled balloons were anchored to each corner, and cloth banners—painted sheets—proclaiming the New Helvetia Jazz Society dangled over the sides, covering the battle scars from Mike's driving.

Although it was still early Friday, throngs of people were already streaming into Old Sacramento. They were being met by dozens of trained volunteer workers—Cheryl and her family among them—who managed the ever-growing crowds with cheerful efficiency. Cheryl's father, who appeared to regard his daughter's suitor with wary approval, had offered to guide the van during the parade as it crept through the crowded streets. That was fortunate for the spectators lining the sidewalks, Meredith thought wryly. If Mike was at the wheel, she never would have allowed herself to be enthroned atop the ancient vehicle.

But her brother and the rest of the band were going to strut alongside while Meredith was supposed to cling to the rusty tiebars and "look pretty." Mostly she thought she must look hot. Despite the capelet sleeves of her crisp white cotton dress, her preferred outfit for daytime performances, she could feel the freckles on her arms bloom-

ing under the noonday sun. She suspected that before the
parade was over her face would have turned into one solid
blotch the color of an old penny. She wished she'd worn a
hat.

She felt very, very conspicuous. One of the guys had
already pointed out a television camera aimed in her
direction, and several jovial passersby had saluted with
paper cups of beer, yelling "Hey, Red, how about some
company up there?"

When she complained, Mike returned, "Honestly, I
don't know what's wrong with you, Merry. The rest of us
are going to have to walk the whole parade route, while
you get to ride." He indicated the TV-news helicopter
hovering overhead. "You'll have by far the best view of
what's going on."

"A lot of good that'll do me," Meredith muttered wasp-
ishly, squinting at the colorful mass of people and vehi-
cles in the staging area. Mike had insisted she wear her
contact lenses during the festival, and most of the activity
around her was a blur. She was particularly disappointed
when a vintage horseless carriage putted by and she could
not clearly see the elderly couple in the back seat, stars
from the big-band era, who were reigning as this year's
emperor and empress of Dixieland.

Suddenly from several blocks away came the loud boom
of a cannon being fired over the Sacramento River. When
the noise ricocheted from the levee banks and echoed
among the high-rise office buildings of the downtown
area, an expectant murmur rumbled through the staging
area. A drum major carrying a cane and spangled top hat
instead of the traditional baton and shako blew cadence
on his whistle, and two young girls hoisting the official
banner of the Dixieland Jubilee between them began to
mark time. Behind them, the first musical unit in the pa-

rade—a brass band from a college in Michigan—joined the count. At a signal the leading row stepped forward and the trumpeter sounded the familiar four-note opening to "When the Saints Go Marching in." The jazz festival was under way. From that point on Meredith's images of the next couple of days' activities were as blurry as her vision.

To manage the hundred-thousand-plus people expected to attend the event, performance sites had to be scattered throughout Sacramento's downtown area. As one of the newest and least-prestigious groups on the program, the New Helvetia Jazz Society had inevitably been booked into the less desirable locations, frequently at awkward times. They played in a stifling circus tent at one o'clock in the afternoon, and in a huge arena set up beneath a freeway overpass . . . during the evening rush hour.

After a while Meredith began to realize that the heat and inconvenience and noise didn't matter. To the jazz fans from throughout the world who converged on the city, everything but the music was irrelevant. All they asked for was a good performance, which they rewarded with cheers and riotous applause. Some audiences literally danced in the aisles. Meredith and her friends gave them their best, and in return they were showered with enthusiasm and even love.

Still, by Saturday evening, as Meredith waited in the wings at Sonora Sue's and the band set up for their set, she wondered if even the audience's unstinting support would be sufficient to help her through the remaining two days of the festival. She was beginning to doubt she had the stamina to carry through to the end. So far she'd sung at seven different shows, with five more yet to come, not counting the Sunday morning gospel sing-along she'd unwisely agreed to join. Her throat was raspy and her wil-

lowy body drooped, making the fringe on the blue silk
flapper dress hang crookedly; the headband she wore was
velvet torture.

Sipping a soft drink, she noted enviously that the band
members seemed to be handling the hectic activity well
enough; they moved around the stage in their spiffy blazers, looking handsome and full of vigor. She'd heard Mike
stagger home at dawn after an all-night jam session with
a quartet from Helsinki, but the lack of sleep didn't seem
to faze him. She wished she had a fraction of his energy.

Suddenly she was poked in the back. A woman's voice
asked archly, "Excuse me, miss. Could you please autograph this program for me?"

Meredith turned, curving her lips into a weary smile.
The smile widened into a genuine grin. "Annette!" she exclaimed with delight. "How long have you been here?"

"I only just barely squeezed in here this minute, but I've
been in Old Sacramento almost continuously since the
parade." She tapped the big blue all-event admission badge
pinned to her shirt. Glancing around the crowded smoky
room, she noted, "I'm really impressed with the way you're
packing them in."

"All these people aren't here for us," Meredith corrected quickly, "it's that band following us, the one made
up of Hollywood actors. We're just the warm-up."

"Well, I guarantee that the people from work have come
to hear *you*," Annette rejoined bracingly. "After we
watched you on the noon news yesterday, I think half the
people at Warcom decided to take off the rest of the afternoon to come down here. I'm surprised you haven't spotted more of them by now."

"With these lousy contacts of mine, I don't see much of
anything," Meredith explained, touched by her friends'
support. "But it's really kind of everyone to take such an

interest. I hope Walter didn't object to people leaving early."

Annette chuckled. "Oh, no, he agreed with us that you're far more entertaining than the average semiconductor, and he said he'd try to get down here himself for at least one of your shows. It's too bad Lois won't make it back from her trip till after the holiday. I know she was looking forward to seeing your group perform. But I did notice Brandt in the audience several times."

Suddenly Meredith felt desolate. He'd been there all along, and she hadn't known. He hadn't cared enough to approach her to congratulate her, or even to critique her performance. Knowing how much of herself she put into her music, the thought of unwittingly exposing her emotions to him while she sang made her feel naked, vulnerable.

"Hasn't Brandt let you know he was here?"

"N-no . . ." Meredith stammered uncomfortably. "He—no." She glanced toward the stage, where the band was in position. "Look, Annette, I have to run," she said. "It's showtime, and it's considered bad form for an opening act to run late and keep the stars waiting. But thanks for stopping by." Waving, she fled to her position beside the piano player.

The set began as usual with an instrumental number, loud and rousing to get the audience's attention. Another quieter instrumental would follow—a piece arranged to showcase the talents of the individual players. Meredith automatically clapped her hands to the beat and waited for her first appearance during the third song. She found herself scanning the crowd in Sonora Sue's, blearily searching for the distinctive flash of light on pale hair as she'd seen it that April Friday.

Had it truly been less than two months since they'd met? Considering how much had happened between them since that initial encounter, the time span seemed much longer. But no, just a few weeks ago she'd still been living in an emotional vacuum, by day trapped in a dead-end job, at night rehearsing with a group of men who were in effect all extensions of her older brother. The jazz festival had been the only point of interest marked on the calendar. Now the festival was here and she was in it, and while part of her exulted at being involved with the commotion and the gaiety and the music, another part of her hated every moment that seemed to separate her from the man she loved.

"Merry."

Mike cleared his throat, and Meredith realized with a start that it was time for her song. As she stood up, she scanned the room one last time. The audience was restive, most of them impatient for the celebrity band that was to follow. Patrons were crammed seven and eight thick around tables meant for couples; more lined the back wall.

When she took her place at the microphone, she squared her shoulders and tossed back her bright hair, ruffling the fringe across her bosom. Someone whistled loudly. Meredith squinted into the darkness, wishing it might be Brandt. But even if she'd been able to see clearly, there was no way she could locate him in this mob. Besides, maybe he wasn't there.

He *might* be there, though, hidden in the shadows of the dim cabaret. The clarinet sounded a high, clear melody line in a minor key and Meredith began to sing. She was singing to Brandt.

She sang of heartbreak and loss, of girls done wrong by fickle lovers, and her voice trembled with the depth of her feelings. When she blended her voice with the woodwind at the end of the tune, stretching the final notes out until the whole room seemed to vibrate with sound, there was a stunned pause. The audience went crazy.

"That concludes the New Helvetia Jazz Society's performance for tonight," Mike breathlessly announced later, tucking his cornet under his arm and mopping his forehead with a soggy handkerchief. The band began to pack their instruments. His words were greeted with loud applause and scattered cries of protest. "Thank you, thank you. You've been a wonderful audience. But now, in just a moment, you're going to hear the group I know you've all been waiting for—"

Meredith slipped off the stage and ducked into the dark hallway leading to the rest rooms. The set had gone remarkably well, but now that the show was over, she felt frazzled, spent. Her eyes burned. She needed sleep.

"Meredith."

She looked up, and it was the first night all over again. Brandt—blond, beautiful, incredibly desirable—towered over her. His jeans clung to his firm thighs, his knit sport shirt outlined the broad muscles of his chest. She remembered the feel of her breasts crushed against those muscles. Despite her fatigue, she had never wanted him as much as she did at that moment. Huskily she whispered, "So you were there, after all."

"Didn't you know? You were staring straight at me most of the—" He broke off and grimaced. Brushing his thumb gently across her cheekbone, he declared, "Oh, yes, the infamous contact lenses. I don't understand why you persist in wearing the stupid things. There's nothing wrong with glasses, any more than there's anything wrong with freckles." His tone softened provocatively. "And, love, you know how I feel about your freckles . . ."

He had said he wanted to kiss every one of them. Meredith shivered deliciously at the memory. "Why don't you give me just a minute to run to the lounge and change—"

"Merry, wait up! Why did you take off like that? There's someone you have to meet!"

Brandt swore under his breath. "Oh, no, not again," Meredith groaned, turning to face her brother as he danced down the hallway toward her. Behind him he was practically dragging a portly middle-aged woman Meredith had never seen before. In their wake trailed the rest of the band.

"This is her!" Mike announced triumphantly, so excited he was almost gibbering. "This is the one we've been waiting for!" He thrust a business card under Meredith's nose.

She could feel Brandt, who was standing just behind her, stiffen as he read the card over her shoulder. With confusion and growing dismay she tried to make out the engraved script:

Cornelia Hatton
Hatton Management, Inc.
Artists' Representative

The address was in the posh Century City district of Los Angeles. Even without that confirmation of the woman's success, however, Meredith would have recognized her name; she was one of the better known agent-managers in the entertainment industry.

So Mike had found his promoter after all. Despite his constant chatter on the subject, Meredith had always thought—hoped—that his vision of being discovered at the jazz festival was a pipe dream. Old Sacramento seemed an unlikely spot to run into big-shot talent scouts.

Mustering a weak smile, Meredith murmured politely, "You're a jazz fan, Ms Hatton?"

"Call me Neil," the other woman responded briskly, shaking hands. "As I was explaining to your brother, I flew up here this weekend as a favor to one of my clients. But when I happened to catch your act . . ." She paused significantly. "I'd really appreciate an opportunity to talk to you, if you have the time."

Meredith's heart lurched. Maybe this was it—the moment she'd prayed would not come, when she'd have to decide whether she was going to sacrifice her own goals in order to fulfill her promise to her brother. She turned her head to glance behind her at Brandt. His expression, which had been warm and full of tenderness moments before, was now closed. Her eyes stinging with unshed tears, she looked at the agent again and began thickly, "Ms Hatton—Neil—I'm not sure—"

"Of course Merry has time to talk!" Mike declared heartily. "Take as long as you want."

The band in the main room of the saloon finished a number, and the raucous applause made conversation in the hallway difficult. "Is there someplace quiet around here?" Neil asked.

Might as well get it over with, Meredith thought resignedly. "I-I was just on my way to the women's lounge," she suggested. She touched Brandt's arm, relishing the softness of the crisp sun-bleached hair. "Please don't go," she whispered. After a moment's hesitation he nodded tersely.

While Meredith removed her irritating lenses, Neil Hatton plopped her ample bottom on the vinyl couch in the corner of the rest room and came to the point. "I was very favorably impressed with your voice, and your stage presence is phenomenal for an amateur—"

"I'm not an amateur," Meredith said, vaguely affronted. "My brother and I have been performing professionally since we were children."

Neil's brows lifted. "I didn't realize that. In any case, in my judgment—and I'm seldom wrong—I think with the proper grooming you have the potential to become a headline artist. If you do decide to take a shot at the big time, I'd like to represent you."

As Meredith settled her glasses on her nose, she asked, "What do you mean by proper grooming?"

"Well, there would have to be cosmetic changes. New costume and makeup, and you'd need to shed about fifteen pounds. It's too bad about the freckles, but I assume they mean your hair color is genuine?"

"Everything about me is genuine," Meredith answered steadily.

Neil nodded. "Excellent. We wouldn't have to start by undoing anyone else's handiwork. Of course, the biggest changes will have to be in your musical style. Although Dixieland and traditional jazz are lovely, they're not particularly in these days. Only established stars can get away with nostalgia, that just makes newcomers seem out-of-date. But I'm sure a competent vocal coach could give you a contemporary commercial sound, and with a good arranger—"

"My brother does all my arrangements."

The agent paused. Regarding Meredith with a calculating gaze, cool and professional, she said deliberately, "I don't want your brother. And if you expect to get anywhere with your career, you won't want him, either."

Meredith grew very still. No, it couldn't be happening this way. If Meredith couldn't take Mike with her, she didn't want to go at all. "But—but my brother and I are a team," she protested. "We always have been. And Mike's work is well thought of in northern California music circles. Why, just recently, on the strength of a single demo tape, an ad agency in San Francisco offered him a job as their in-house composer."

"Then I'd advise him to take it," Neil said bluntly. "He may be a fair musician, but you're the one with star quality. You have a spark about you that's very rare. Cultivated properly, you could go to the top. But your family and friends would be only so much dead wood, cluttering up your life. Clear them out."

"And if I don't want to clear them out?"

Neil leaned forward. "Then you'll never make it, not with my agency, anyway. If an artist isn't willing to devote herself solely to her career, then I won't waste my time with her. Maybe I sound harsh, even cruel, but believe me, I've seen too many promising performers impeded by some misguided loyalty to no-talent hangers-on—"

Behind her glasses Meredith's eyes glittered. "There are some people who still think loyalty and friendship are more important than being a star."

"There are some people who still think Nixon was not a crook," Neil countered. She pulled a pack of cigarettes from her handbag and fidgeted with the lighter. Squinting at the flame, she muttered, "My dear, do you realize that propositions like mine don't come along every day? Clients seek me out, not vice versa. No matter how talented you are, you may never get another offer."

"I think I know what I'm turning down," Meredith said.

The agent studied her curiously. Gradually her cynical expression softened, and she muttered, "Maybe you do at that. Maybe you do . . . I just hope you don't regret your decision later."

"Believe me, I won't."

"Oh, well," Neil said, sighing, "whatever happens, I wish you luck. I really did enjoy your singing."

The two women parted gravely, and with leaden footsteps Meredith made her way back to the main room of the cabaret. Brandt, Mike and the others were waiting. She did not know where—or if—she was going to find the courage to tell her brother his glowing dreams had all been shattered.

"Hey, Merry, what took you so long?" Mike demanded, drawing reproving scowls from the crowd watching the group on the stage. Grudgingly he lowered his voice. "What happened?" he whispered hoarsely. "Where's Ms Hatton?"

"She's gone," Meredith stated simply.

"What do you mean, she's gone?"

The band members exchanged glances, then Don piped up, "You know, Mike, I think I'd like to stretch my legs a little. I'm going to head on out of here now. I'll see you later at the jam session." The other musicians swiftly followed him.

Following the band's abrupt departure, Brandt studied the two siblings. Meredith's face looked pinched, her freckles stood out against her pallid cheeks, her head drooped like a flower on a broken stem. Whatever the agent had said to her, it had upset her badly. On the other hand, Mike's glower was growing darker, as if a storm was building inside him. The jerk—couldn't he tell something was wrong with his sister?

With tact that Brandt acknowledged was uncharacteristic of himself, he suggested, "Why don't we continue this discussion outside, where it's not so loud and stuffy?" Before anyone could protest, he slipped his arm around

Meredith's shoulders and ushered her toward the door. She was trembling violently.

Elbowing a path through the crowd of spectators bunched around the exit of Sonora Sue's, Brandt led Meredith and her brother across the Embarcadero. The street had been cordoned off for the festival, and they passed a clean-up crew sweeping away the trash that littered the cobbled pavement. Tired jazz fans perched atop the floodwall, watching the moonlit river, or strolled along the levee in pairs and groups. Music drifted on the sultry night air from a dozen different locations; an elderly couple danced on the sidewalk, jitterbugging to a distant tune. Apart from someone who waved a boozy but cordial greeting as they passed, nobody paid attention to the three people stalking purposefully toward the relative privacy of the dark wall.

When they found a spot quiet enough to talk, Mike whirled on his sister and demanded, "All right, tell me what happened with the Hatton woman. Is this our big break? Did she like us? Did she talk about taking us on as clients?"

Smiling ironically, Meredith said, "She told me I could be a star."

"Well, of course!" Mike crowed with delight, almost incoherent in his rapture. "God, Merry, you had me worried there for a minute! So what plans did you make? What happens next? When do we head off for the big time?"

She hesitated, still uncertain how to explain what had occurred without cruelly crushing her brother. She looked up at Brandt. His eyes were shadowed and unfathomable, but she could feel the tension stiffening his long, lean body. He seemed to be awaiting her reply as anxiously as Mike was. Returning her gaze to her brother, Meredith gulped and tried to moisten her mouth; her tongue felt like suede.

Clasping his arm, she said gently, "We aren't going anywhere, Mike. I turned her down."

In the pulsing silence that followed, Mike was too flabbergasted to do more than gape, his jaw slack with shock. But Brandt pressed, "Why, Meredith? Why did you reject the agent's offer?"

After the way I sang for you, don't you know? Meredith stared at Brandt, her silent plea written on her face. The thought that he could still doubt her sincerity was so painful that tears welled in her eyes. Blinking, she asked plaintively, "Have you forgotten my promise to remain at Warcom? You really need someone to evaluate all those computer readouts for you, you know. I told you I wouldn't leave you in the lurch the way your last assistant did."

Mike finally recovered his voice. Brushing away his sister's reassuring caress, he rounded on Brandt and grated, "Listen, Dahlberg, I don't know what this hold is that you have over my sister—"

"Love?" Brandt offered mildly, making Meredith's heart flip.

"Love?" Mike sneered. "What do you know about love? Love is caring and looking after someone, the way I've done ever since Merry was a baby. All you've ever seemed to do for her is make her cry."

Dashing aside the wetness beading her lashes, Meredith protested, "Please, Mike, don't—"

"Now, wait a minute, Forrester—"

Ignoring them, Mike railed, "Damn you, Dahlberg, look at her! She was perfectly content until she met you, but now you've got her torn into little pieces. Tonight is the moment she's been waiting for all her life, maybe her one shot at catching the brass ring, and you are holding her back! If what you feel for her is really love, then for God's sake, man, let her go!"

Brandt looked thunderstruck. Wedging herself between the two men, Meredith clutched at Brandt's shirt, pinching star-shaped creases into the soft fabric. "Don't listen to Mike," she begged. "He's wrong. I don't want to be a star, I just want to be with you."

Splaying his callused fingertips delicately across her mouth, Brandt silenced her. "Hush, Merry Forrest," he crooned. "It's all right. I do understand."

"No, you don't," she insisted desperately, ignoring his gesture. "I want to live with you, after all. I'm sorry I turned you down when you asked me before. I want to be with you, work with you—"

Just for a moment his fingers pressed more firmly over her lips, absorbing their satin moisture. Then he dropped his hand and shook his head slowly. "But you can't work with me anymore. You're fired."

With a curt nod he turned and stalked away, back across the cobbled street to the sidewalk outside Sonora Sue's. Meredith watched helplessly as he disappeared into the dancing crowd.

"I-I'm sorry, Merry," Mike said, clumsily trying to hug his sister. "I know you're feeling bad, but believe me, it'll get better."

She shrugged him off. "I will never forgive you for this, ever," she said. Her voice was as dull as her eyes.

"Yes, you will. You're confused right now, but once we've made our start, you'll be happy again. So why don't we go track down the Hatton woman? I can still hear the celebrity band playing, so she's probably in the area. We'll just tell her you were so startled by her offer that at first you didn't know what you were saying. I'm sure she'll understand."

"No."

Mike's tone sharpened. "Meredith, you have to talk to the agent. You promised."

Her shoulders slumped. Suddenly she was too tired to maintain any pretense of tact. "I did talk to Neil Hatton about you," she informed her brother drearily, "and she doesn't want you. She says you're not good enough."

"Not good enough?" Mike echoed indignantly, choking on the words. "What the hell does she mean by that? I've been performing all my life!"

Meredith sighed. "She says you're fine for the kind of gigs you and the band are already doing, but she doesn't feel you have the talent for the big time. Right or wrong, she's not interested in representing you, and I told her I wasn't interested in signing up without you."

"So because some Hollywood bitch decrees I don't meet her elevated standards," Mike demanded bitterly, "you and I are condemned to play in dives the rest of our lives, the way Mom and Dad did?"

Lifting her chin, Meredith regarded her brother steadily. "Once the Jubilee is over, I will never perform again."

"Merry—" Mike started to protest, but seeing her resolute expression, he broke off. "Lord," he muttered in wonder, "you really mean it."

"Damn right I do."

"And what about me?" he persisted. "Where am I supposed to go without you?"

"I don't know, but if you're wise you'll follow your heart. Start living life for yourself, and not because you think you have to fulfill some phantom obligation to our parents."

"But they worked so hard, Merry, and they never made it—"

"But were they unhappy?" Meredith rejoined. "You know I hated the way Mom and Dad dragged us around the country. But despite all the insecurity, the constant uprooting, do you think *they* were unhappy with their life?"

Mike's brow wrinkled. "Well, no, I guess not," he conceded.

"But why not? According to you, they never got the thing they wanted most out of life. Why weren't they miserable and frustrated?"

Again Mike scowled. Then with an air of discovery he exclaimed, "They had each other. Till the day they died, they were in love. Maybe in the final analysis nothing else was ever as important to them as that."

"Exactly," Meredith said. "And don't you think they'd agree it's time you forgot about pursuing their dreams and concentrate on making a life for yourself and the girl you claim you love? Think of the possibilities if you branch out in another direction. We both know you're a much better arranger and composer than you are a performer. You could see if that job in San Francisco is still open. If you don't like the idea of working in advertising then look for something else."

"Those Finnish guys I was sitting in with last night did say something about buying some of my charts," Mike admitted diffidently. "They seemed quite impressed with them."

"Well, there you are. Start composing in earnest."

Her brother flashed a whimsical smile. "I think I'd like that. There are a lot of tunes in my head that I've never written down, mostly because they weren't suitable for the band."

"Maybe it's time for you to break away from the band, too."

Mike looked astonished. "But I founded that band! It's been part of my life since I was a kid."

"And you're not a kid anymore. You've outgrown it." Meredith touched his arm reassuringly. "Don't worry, Mike. I think the guys would understand."

He nodded silently. Meredith watched him gnaw his lip as he considered what she'd said. "Songwriting's not exactly an easy field to break into," he mused. "It could take time."

"But you have time. Cheryl's only eighteen. It would probably be better if the two of you held off until she finishes college before you seriously consider marriage. And while you're waiting for her, you could compose, you could teach, you could travel the way you planned to before Mom and Dad died. I'd help out."

"I think you've already helped out enough, sis," Mike said. "If I'm going to take care of a wife, I'd better get busy taking care of myself." He gazed at Meredith with bemused affection. "You know, for a baby sister, you can be downright profound at times."

"It's just common sense."

His tone darkened. "Merry, hon, have I messed up your life by spoiling things for you and Brandt?"

She shook her head. "No, Mike. The fault is mine, for being such a wimp. I never should have allowed myself to be put into a position where I had to choose between you and Brandt. Oh, well, now it's too late." She glanced at her wristwatch. "And speaking of late—you'd better hurry if you're going to make it to your jam session on time. And I need to head home and get some sleep. That gospel sing-along starts at eight in the morning."

HER NAME WAS still painted on the bumper at the end of her parking space, Meredith noted with relief. She steered her Toyota into the spot next to Brandt's vacant one. Considering how quickly the inscription had appeared when she began work at Warcom, she'd been afraid it would simply vanish now that she'd been fired. But no, for the moment M. Forrester still lay alongside B. Dahlberg, joined in concrete if not in flesh. She supposed because of the three-day weekend he must not yet have had an opportunity to inform the maintenance staff of her altered status.

Switching off the engine, Meredith leaned back in her seat and shifted uncomfortably, smoothing down the narrow skirt of her beige business suit where it had ridden high up on her thighs while she drove. After weeks of dressing casually for work, the flannel fabric felt hot and binding, but she had resumed the formal gear with a purpose.

As soon as she cleaned out her desk and collected her severance pay, she intended to drive around to the other high-tech firms in the Sacramento area and leave employment applications. Although she had a depressing premonition that her abrupt dismissal from Warcom was going to make it harder than ever for her to secure the kind of work she wanted, she had to try. She needed a job.

Just as she reminded herself sternly that she could not afford to waste time brooding, the man she was brooding about zoomed past her car on his ten-speed. Meredith spotted him as his helmeted reflection flashed across her rearview mirror, and she turned in her seat in time to watch him skid to a halt in front of the security guard's station. He did not glance in her direction.

She watched as his long bronzed leg swung gracefully as he dismounted. His taut buttocks were cupped by his skimpy shorts as he squatted to thread a cable through the sprocket wheel and lock it around the bike racks. Hunger wrenched at Meredith and she sighed dispiritedly. She knew every centimeter of that beautiful body, every movement of those strong, wonderfully controlled muscles. She did not know if her craving for him would ever ease.

As she stepped out of her car, she was greeted by a couple from the engineering division, who told her they'd spotted her on television when a local news program broadcast excerpts from Friday's parade. By the time they finished chatting about the jazz festival, Brandt had disappeared from view.

The B-natural chime on the elevator sounded a little flat, Meredith noted, as the doors swished open on the fifth floor—or perhaps it was only her own mood that was flat. None of the other employees stepping into the lushly carpeted corridor with her seemed to notice anything amiss. On the contrary, they were all chipper and bubbly, well rested after the long weekend. Several told Meredith they'd seen her perform. She accepted their compliments with a smile, realizing once again that Brandt wasn't the only person at Warcom she regretted leaving.

She could hear the sound of Brandt's shower pulsing through the pipes in the walls as she passed her own office without stopping. Lois would be back from her trip to

Mexico by now, and as she had been the first person Meredith had met at Warcom, she wanted Lois to be the first person to whom she said goodbye.

Stepping through the double doors at the end of the hallway, Meredith met with a surprise. "Oh, great!" Lois greeted her, "I was going to come looking for you, to say goodbye before I leave."

"Leave?" Meredith echoed blankly. She realized Lois was carefully wrapping tissue around the small potted African violet that sat beside her word processor. The rest of her desk looked empty, stripped of personal belongings. "But you just got back."

"And now I'm going again. I've got a new job, a management position this time. No more typing letters and keeping phone logs for me!"

"Oh, Lois, that's wonderful," Meredith enthused, noting the way her friend's face glowed with pride and excitement. "Where is the job? Tell me all about it."

"Well, it's a new firm in Phoenix—"

"Arizona?"

Lois grinned. "Yes. I met this man on the boat, a widower who's decided to start his own video equipment business now that his two children are grown. He convinced me that the Sunbelt is where it's all happening today."

Meredith suddenly remembered the unidentified tourist in the snapshot Lois had sent her. So that was why she'd looked as if she were blossoming. Glancing toward the closed door to Walter's office, she said quietly, "But, Lois, I thought it was already happening here."

The older woman's smile faded. "*Nothing* was happening here." After a moment her expression softened, and she said gently, "Look, honey, it's not just personal, it's more than simply meeting a new man. I had a great time with him on the cruise, but it's far too early to tell whether anything permanent will ever develop between us. But one thing he did for me was make me realize that I'm still in my prime. I'm forty-six years old, and even if that may sound ancient to a young woman like you, I know I've got lots of productive years ahead of me yet. And I refuse to waste any more of them stagnating in a job—and a personal relationship—that, bluntly, have no further opportunity for advancement!"

Meredith regarded Lois acutely. Despite the woman's obvious pleasure and anticipation, she sensed lingering regret, too. "I'm very happy for you, Lois, but I know that can't have been an easy decision for you to make."

"I never said it was easy." Lois stared down at the violet she was wrapping. Suddenly she picked up the plant and thrust it at Meredith. "Here, honey, why don't you keep this? I just remembered I won't be able to carry it across the state line into Arizona, anyway." As Meredith murmured her thanks, Lois glanced at Walter's door. "Be nice to him, won't you? I think I'll head down the hall and talk to Annette for a while."

After Lois left the room, Meredith suddenly realized she could make out music and other noise filtering through Walter's door. Rapping her knuckles on the heavy wood, she heard a deep voice croak, "Who is it?" After Meredith identified herself, there was a long pause. "Come on in." The voice was still gruff.

"Thank you. Mr. Warren, I—" Meredith stopped in midsentence, too shocked to speak.

Every mechanical toy and gadget in the room was in operation. Windup cars raced in circles around the floor. On the desk a furry monkey pounded a drum and blew bubbles. A robot with flashlight bulbs for eyes was stalled against the telephone, whirring and blinking in electric frustration. The delightful antique nickelodeon played "Hail, Hail, the Gang's All Here" at full blast. The racket was unbearable.

In the midst of the commotion stood Walter, his bright intelligent eyes dim above his bushy beard, his huge body looking shrunken, almost wizened. He clutched a sheet of typed paper—no doubt a letter of resignation.

Quickly Meredith moved through the room, switching off toys and noisemakers. When the motor on the nickelodeon ran down, stilling the bellows, the room was silent again. She sighed. "Oh, Walter, I'm so sorry."

He shook his head, his expression bitter. "Don't pity me, girl. I'm just a gutless old man who's suffering because I was too wishy-washy—or selfish—to resolve my private life. I've always wanted things both ways, *my* way. Even now, when it might be my very last chance to straighten things out, I found I just couldn't say I'd get a divorce."

"There's nothing wrong with being loyal to your wife, sir."

"There is if I use it as an excuse to string Lois along." Walter snorted. "She's a fine woman. She deserves better. Oh, hell, whatever happens in Phoenix, I hope she's happy."

His rumbling voice subsided into ruminative silence, and after a moment Meredith asked, "Is there anything I can do for you?"

"No, my dear," he murmured, not looking at her. "But thank you for your concern."

Meredith hesitated awkwardly. "Well, if you're sure you'll be all right, then . . . then I guess I'd better be leaving. I just wanted to say goodbye before I headed down to personnel to pick up my check."

Walter's head jerked up. "Goodbye? Check? What are you talking about?"

Licking her dry lips, Meredith explained, "I'm leaving Warcom. Brandt fired me."

"Fired you? Why on earth would that idiot boy want to do a thing like that? I've been holding my breath for weeks, waiting for you two to announce your engagement!"

Meredith said steadily, "Marriage has never been mentioned between Brandt and me, Walter. In any case, our personal relationship has nothing to do with his decision. Apparently Brandt feels that my moonlighting as a singer is having a detrimental effect on my work here at Warcom—"

"That's a crock," Walter cut in impatiently. "You're the best PA he's ever had."

"Thanks. I wish Brandt agreed with you. Unfortunately, he says I have to make a decision as to which direction I want to take my career."

"And being Brandt, he has then proceeded to make the decision for you?" Walter judged acutely.

Meredith grimaced. "He refuses to believe that mathematics is my field of choice. He—and to be fair, most other people—just naturally assume I'd rather be in show business. Nobody seems to understand that I've already been in show business, and I don't like it."

"Have you told Brandt how you feel?"

"Repeatedly. I might as well be talking to his bicycle." Meredith clucked glumly. "Anyway, it's too late to change his mind now."

"No!" Walter barked. He waved the letter at Meredith. "Listen here, young lady. This is too late! But as long as you and Brandt Dahlberg are both alive and unattached, there's still hope. And if you're half as fiery as that hair of yours, you'll march right down to his office and convince him once and for all that you know what's good for you. If not—"

He faltered. His shoulders hunched and his seamed face suddenly appeared old and defenseless. "Meredith, my dear," he suggested tentatively, "if Brandt won't listen to reason, well . . . I'm going to have to find someone to replace Lois."

Smiling tenderly, Meredith rounded the desk and kissed his bald head. "Thank you very much for the offer, boss. Somehow, though, I doubt anyone is ever going to replace Lois for you."

He patted her hand. "No, probably not." Gesturing toward the outer office, he grumbled, "Now get on out of here—scoot, shoo! Quick, before I embarrass myself."

Meredith scampered away. When she reached the door, Walter called, "Oh, and Ms Forrester—"

At the lift in his voice, she paused, glancing back over her shoulder. "Sir?"

Walter grinned wickedly. "Meredith, when you and that partner of mine have your little talk, remember to lock the office door."

BRANDT CRANKED the shower tap counterclockwise until it was wide open, but the water gushing over his body, stinging like electric needles, refused to grow hotter. He swore with frustration. His skin glowed from the force of the spray, but right now he wanted the water to be scalding hot, blistering hot, hot enough to sear away the images that tormented him.

Meredith. He kept remembering the anguished look in her eyes when last he'd seen her. He remembered another time, too, when her eyes had been wild and green-gold in the afternoon sunlight, as she tossed her head back and forth on lavender-scented linen.

Oh, hell, maybe the idea of laving away thoughts of her was self-defeating. Heat and moisture and herbal soap smelling like the smoky-sweet grasses that had clung to her body that day on the bike trail all mingled into a heady mixture. Brandt ground his teeth to keep from groaning.

Definitely time to get out, he decreed with a disgruntled snort. His skin was beginning to wrinkle. He was a businessman, after all, and he had work to do. Item one on the agenda was to politely ask Annette Nakatani if she could spare one of her precious lambs to deal with routine clerical matters. Then he had to locate a person who could also handle the more abstruse interpretive functions required of his assistant. Item one-a, he amended wryly, was to convince Annette he would not turn into a werewolf or something when said lamb proved unable to spell.

Throwing back his head so that the spray hit his Adam's apple, Brandt rinsed away the last dregs of soap and turned off the stream of water. He combed his hair away from his face with his fingers, straining out the wetness, and wiped his dripping mustache with the back of his hand. Pushing open the fogged glass door, he groped blindly for a towel. The shelf was empty.

"You know, if you stay in the shower too long, you're liable to wash away all your natural oils."

Brandt started. Meredith was leaning against the door, his terry bathrobe on a hook behind her. Her mouth was curved faintly, her eyes alight with smug amusement. He noted curiously that her hair was scraped into one of those tight French twists he disliked, and she was dressed in the formal business suit she had worn when she first came to Warcom. In her arms she was holding all the towels.

"Uh, hello," Brandt said blankly. Water dripped off his head and beaded on his shoulders in cool drops that tickled as they continued their slide down his clammy skin. He watched Meredith's eyes follow the course of rivulets that trickled from his neck and chest to pool in the thatch of curly dark-blond hair at his loins. Unwillingly his body stirred, stimulated by her inspection. When she did not speak, he shivered and asked with spurious calm, "Will you hand me my robe, please?"

Meredith shook her head. Brandt's tone sharpened. "At least give me something to dry off with, then."

"No."

He stepped toward her, bare feet squishing on the sodden bath mat. As she was backed against the door, Meredith could not retreat, but her arms tightened protectively around the bundle of towels. He had the odd feeling he'd have to wrest them from her by force. Halting, he snapped impatiently, "Damn it, Meredith, stop playing games. I'm cold!"

Her smile remained imperturbable, but something flickered in her eyes. She took a deep breath. "I'm sorry you're cold," she said, her tone noticeably unrepentant, "but at least this way, as long as I have the towels, I know I also have your attention. And you and I need to talk. I want some explanations."

He felt like a fool. "Confound it, woman, I don't have to explain anything to you!"

Meredith's brows lifted. "Don't bluster, darling," she chided mildly. "It doesn't work when you're naked."

Brandt blushed. He did not think he had blushed since the seventh grade, the day his shorts split during a coed gymnastics class, but he still recognized the feeling. Telltale heat rouged his cheeks and seeped under his tan like lava moving just beneath the crust of the earth. He gritted his teeth in embarrassment and dismay, helpless to halt the inexorable rise of color.

After a moment Meredith took pity on him. "Here," she said, handing over his robe. "But please, promise me that once you've put it on, you'll still listen to what I have to say."

Grudgingly Brandt nodded his assent. Meredith set the stack of towels on the edge of the sink and left the bathroom.

He was almost as sexy in that robe as he was nude, she decided, when Brandt followed her into his office. From where she sat at one end of the couch, she had a tantalizing view of his powerful thigh muscles almost to the juncture of his legs as he stalked across the room, the robe flapping open just above his knees. Meredith was reminded of some Olympian deity. She'd never been especially enamored of the Greek gods—most of them seemed a bit effete for her tastes—but if any had looked like Brandt, then she could well understand why all those shepherd maidens had surrendered their virtue at the drop of a laurel leaf.

"Meredith, why are you here?"

Looming over her, he seemed genuinely puzzled. Meredith craned her neck and regarded him quizzically. "Maybe I want you to write me a letter of reference for my next job."

"A reference from me won't be of much use to a singer."

"I am not a singer," she said deliberately. "The Dixieland Jubilee marked the final appearance of Merry Forrest, alone or with the band. I have retired."

"Oh, really? What about your brother?"

"Mike and I have decided it's time for us to go our separate ways."

"Just like that?"

"Just like that."

Brandt plopped onto the end of the sofa opposite her. "I don't believe you. Why have you retired?"

"Because I'm not interested in performing anymore, that's why."

He sniffed skeptically. "I find it a little hard to accept your sudden lack of interest when your whole life seems to revolve around the stage and your brother's jazz band. I can't see you or even telephone you at your apartment without our being interrupted by him or a herd of rowdy musicians."

"Well, maybe I'm fed up with the lack of privacy, too. Have you thought of that?" Meredith tossed back. "Or maybe I'm just fed up, period. Don't you think burnout is reason enough to give up music?"

"Of course it is," he said grimly, "as long as you're sure it's the real reason. I will not allow you to throw away your talents because you're in love with me and you think it's what I want you to do!"

Meredith grew very still, but behind her glasses her lashes fluttered like birds beating against a windowpane. "Are you telling me," she queried dangerously, "that you fired me for my own good?"

He shifted uncomfortably. Combing his mustache with his knuckles, he muttered, "I did what I thought was best."

Closing her eyes completely, Meredith counted to ten, which did no good; by twenty she was furious. She exploded. "Damn you, Brandt Dahlberg, your nobility of purpose would be quite touching if it weren't so incredibly conceited! Who gave you the right to analyze my motives? Yes, I love you, but that doesn't mean my brain has turned to tapioca! Where the hell do you get off assuming I'm going to surrender my personhood?"

"I have never made any assumptions about your personhood," Brandt denied. "Wanting what's best for you does not mean I don't respect your right to make decisions."

"Then why do you pigheadedly refuse to respect my decision to quit singing?" Meredith cried. "Why are you so certain I'm lying about what I want just to please you?"

"Because, goddamnit," Brandt retorted through clenched teeth, "that's exactly what I did twelve years ago!"

Meredith collapsed back against the arm of the couch and stared in confusion. Beneath the water-darkened fall of hair plastered against his forehead, Brandt's face was ashen. "I don't understand. Are you talking about your wife?"

Brandt made an impatient gesture. "No, of course not. This has nothing to do with her, at least not directly. I've told you, the misery she and I wrought on each other was an outgrowth of the real problem: the way I gave up my plans to become a professional cyclist in order to please my father and Walter."

When Meredith did not speak, Brandt continued with a sigh. "You know how you've told me about your family pushing you onto the stage at an early age? Maybe you don't realize yet that a very similar thing happened to me.

In my case, Walter and my dad pushed me into Warcom. When they first teamed up Walter was a self-trained scientist fascinated by the new field of solid-state electronics, my father was a young businessman with an infant son to raise. My mother had died very early of a congenital heart weakness, which I suppose is one of the reasons I've always been so concerned with keeping physically fit. Walter was married, but his wife didn't seem to like kids very much. In retrospect I'm sure she was already ill. In any case, the two men teamed up, and Walter became my jovial godfather who was always bringing me marvelous toys. Together they raised me with the idea that someday I'd inherit the company they built."

Brandt's voice grew soft, and for a moment he gazed pensively at the glass case filled with his athletic trophies. "I never questioned their plans until I got into college. To please them I majored in computer technology and business administration and did acceptably well. But when I became involved in cycling, I discovered a whole new world—*my* world, a world in which I not only did acceptably well, I was damned good! I wanted to stay in that world."

He shook his head wryly. "Of course I realized Dad and Walter expected me to join the firm just as soon as I graduated, but what I did *not* realize was the uproar that would ensue when I hinted I'd like to join the European circuit for a while. For the first time in my life, my father and I actually yelled at each other. His anger hurt. Finally he threatened to disinherit me—a heavy threat indeed to a spoiled kid who's had everything he's ever wanted handed to him on a platter!"

Hearing the strain in Brandt's voice, Meredith tried to console him. "But surely he didn't mean that."

Brandt shrugged. "I'll never know. A few weeks later, while things were still tense between us, Dad had a stroke. Even though the doctors assured me he'd been building up to the attack for a long time, I felt guilty, as if it was all my fault for having dared argue with him. He died begging for reassurance that I didn't hate him for pressuring me to join the family business. He had only acted out of love. So naturally I told him—and Walter, too—that my interest in cycling had been a momentary aberration and that what I really and truly wanted out of life was to work in the electronics industry."

The room was silent for a moment. Then Meredith said simply, "I'm sorry, Brandt. I thought you were happy at Warcom."

"I am happy at Warcom. As a matter of fact," he admitted, "the work has turned out to be challenging and fulfilling and far more enjoyable than I ever imagined when I was twenty-one. Even if it hadn't been, the odds are I would have ended up working here eventually, after my knees gave out or, hopefully, after I retired in triumph from the racing circuit."

His ironic smile faded. "But that's not the point, Meredith. The point is that I never had a chance to find out whether I could have been a champion. Maybe that sounds like a frivolous ambition, but in the beginning my resentment over being denied the chance was fierce enough to drive me into a disastrous marriage, just out of spite. I've grown up since then, I don't actively resent what happened anymore, but I do know the uncertainty is going to nag me for the rest of my life. And that's the kind of regret I wanted to spare you."

"I will never regret getting out of show business."

"Are you sure?" He stretched his arm along the back of the sofa beckoningly. Meredith wound her fingers through his. Her skin tingled at his touch, and suddenly the prim business suit felt intolerably tight; she couldn't breathe. She began to toy with the buttons on the jacket. Unaware of her discomfort, Brandt continued earnestly, his eyes darkening. "You're very talented, you know, but even more than that, you have a presence. Friday, when everyone in the office was clustered around the television to watch the parade on the noon news, people commented on the way you dominated the camera whenever it was pointed in your direction. With the sun on your hair, you looked so beautiful and vibrant that it seemed as if you were going to burn right through the picture tube."

"Probably just the dress." Meredith dismissed his flattery. "I understand white drives TV cameramen wild."

Squeezing her hand, Brandt reproached, "Don't be glib, Meredith. I'm serious about this. It wasn't just your friends here at Warcom who noticed your star quality. Even sitting on top of that silly van the way you were, the crowd in Old Sacramento cheered as if you were a princess greeting her adoring subjects. Their response reminded me a little of the spectators lining the route of the Brevet, the time I raced in Switzerland. I remember how seductive that kind of adulation can be. It's not an easy thing to give up."

"But I'm not interested in adulation," she insisted, "only love."

"You know I love you."

She inhaled shakily. Her probing gaze locked with his, anxious yet hopeful. "Do you love me enough to step back and let me decide for myself what I want out of life?"

"Well, surely that depends on—" He choked off his automatic response. "Of course," he agreed. "You can have anything you want."

"Thank you."

Nervously Meredith picked at the pins securing her hair. She didn't know what to say. Brandt watched in silence as one long flaming strand after another fell free and feathered softly around her face. At last he asked whimsically, "Darling, would it be a flagrant violation of your personhood if I were to inquire exactly what it is you do want?"

"Of course not. I want a career in mathematics—"

"You have it," Brandt agreed at once, "here at Warcom. Or if you get tired of working for me, you can get a job anywhere you wish. For that matter, if you want to go back to college and finish up your degree, that could probably be arranged, too."

Meredith gasped with delight. "Oh, Brandt, I hadn't even thought of returning to school! That would be wonderful."

He nodded. "Anything else?"

This time her response was a little less flippant, a little more wistful. "I want a normal, stable home life, in some sort of permanent surroundings—"

"You've never seen my house, have you? It's on a bluff overlooking the American River. I think you'll like it."

Her lips trembled and, brushing back a strand of hair that dangled over her eyes, she stared at the floor. "You want me to move in with you?" she murmured.

"Actually," he said quietly, touching her chin, lifting it so that she had to look directly at him, "today happens to be the last day of May, and I was thinking—what could be more normal than a June wedding? We could even hire your brother's band for the reception."

"Oh, Brandt!" Meredith's face lit up with sheer blazing joy. Giddily she flung herself into his arms.

They tumbled backward onto the broad leather couch, and heated moments passed while their clothing was dispatched and the last of her hairpins was tossed aside. Brandt paused long enough to ask seriously one last time, "Darling, are you sure you won't miss singing?"

"Idiot," she replied. She gazed with passion-glazed eyes at the golden body beneath her, felt her softness against his fiercely aroused strength. She laced her fingers through the pale silky hair at his temples. Her breath ruffled his mustache as she whispered, "You still don't know, do you?" Then her lips met his, and she set out to prove that in his arms she would always sing.

Harlequin Temptation

COMING NEXT MONTH

HARLEQUIN HISTORICAL

Explore love with Harlequin in the Middle
Ages, the Renaissance, in the Regency, the
Victorian and other eras.

Relive within these books the endless ages of
romance, set against authentic historical
backgrounds. Two new historical love stories
published each month.

HIST-B-1

Take 4 best-selling love stories FREE
Plus get a FREE surprise gift!

PATRICIA MATTHEWS

America's First Lady of Romance upholds her long standing reputation as a bestselling romance novelist with . . .

Enchanted

Caught in the steamy heat of America's New South, Rebecca Trenton finds herself torn between two brothers—she yearns for one but a dark secret binds her to the other.

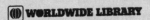

ATTRACTIVE, SPACE SAVING BOOK RACK

Display your most prized novels on this handsome and sturdy book rack. The hand-rubbed walnut finish will blend into your library decor with quiet elegance, providing a practical organizer for your favorite hard-or soft-covered books.

Only $9.95

Approximately 16" x 8" when assembled

Assembles in seconds!

To order, rush your name, address and zip code, along with a check or money order for $10.70* ($9.95 plus 75¢ postage and handling) payable to *Harlequin Reader Service*:

Harlequin Reader Service
Book Rack Offer
901 Fuhrmann Blvd.
P.O. Box 1325
Buffalo, NY 14269-1325

Offer not available in Canada.

*New York residents add appropriate sales tax.

BKR-1R